Praise for *Choices*

"Jacquelyn Lynn has a unique God-given talent that glistens in this amazing work. The story is captivating and keeps you in a state of wonderful wonder." – *Don Abbott*

"I just could not put it down. Love the characters." – *Kim R.*

"I kept asking myself what I would do as any of the characters. They were all so relatable and the range of emotions was believable and engrossing." – *Virginia B.*

"There are times when you just can't put a book down – and this was one of them! Jacquelyn Lynn masterfully wove the stories of several individuals to show how forgiveness for yourself and others is possible even in the darkest of circumstances." - *Mark Goldstein*

"I have not enjoyed a book like I enjoyed this one in a long time." – *Joanna L.*

"It was awesome! The heart and passion and soul of the characters spoke to me loudest. Each character was truly brought to life in an emotional way and took a toll on my heart and mind. There were twists and turns I did not expect. I thought I knew what was coming next, but I was surprised throughout." – *Jack Alan Levine*

"Little did I know the story would have such an impact on me. I couldn't put it down." – *Brenda S.*

Choices

Inspirational Books by Jacquelyn Lynn

Finding Joy in the Morning: You can make it through the night

Words to Work By: 31 devotions for the workplace based on the Book of Proverbs

A Joyful Cup Story

Choices

Jacquelyn Lynn

Tuscawilla Creative Services
CreateTeachInspire.com

Library of Congress Control Number: 2019903469

ISBN: 978-1-941826-28-7

To Alan

9
11. Do you need police, fire, or medical?"

"A car hit a bicycle. The guy on the bike bounced over the car. They just drove away."

The caller was breathless as he ran toward the bleeding man lying on the road, his footsteps echoing in the stillness. His headlights pierced the pre-dawn darkness, shining like a spotlight on a sickening scene that was in stark contrast to the sweet night air and a world that was beginning to wake up.

"What is your location?" The dispatcher's voice was cool, crisp, almost detached.

"Not sure. I'm on State Road 434. Heading west."

"What's the last thing you remember passing?"

"An apartment complex. I'm on that stretch where it's just woods. No street lights." He scanned the area for landmarks that would help.

"Are you near the pedestrian overpass?"

"I think so. I haven't passed it yet. I'm east of it. Not far." Holding his phone in one hand, he pulled off his jacket with the other, knelt next to the cyclist, and covered the injured man's torso.

"The police are on their way." The dispatcher's voice was reassuring. "Are you with the person who was hit?"

"Yes."

"I'm going to transfer you to Fire Rescue. Stay on the line, sir. Do not hang up."

"Okay."

After a few endless seconds, another brisk voice came on the line. "Fire Rescue."

The 911 dispatcher responded efficiently. "Police are en route to a car versus bicycle with injuries. Caller does not have an exact location. They are on State Road 434 approximately one-half mile east of the pedestrian overpass."

"Got it. Caller, this is Fire Rescue. What is your location?"

"What? I gave my location to the other operator. This guy needs help. Now!"

"I understand, sir. We need to be sure we know where you are so we can get people there to assist you." The Fire Rescue dispatcher was calm, dispassionate.

"I'm on 434, heading west. I'm just past the large apartment complex that's the last one before the woods. On the north side of the street. My car's in the right lane with the headlights and emergency flashers on. It's a white Ford mustang." A car drove past in the left lane, slowed, then accelerated, its taillights fading in the distance.

"Are you with the victim?"

"Yes."

"Is he conscious?"

"No. I don't think so. His eyes are closed. He's got a helmet on but his face is bloody and he's moaning. Hey, fella, can you hear me?" A pause. "He's not responding."

"But he's breathing?"

"Yes." The injured man's chest rose and fell with each shallow breath. In the distance, a siren wailed, growing louder as the emergency vehicle approached. "Dude, can you hear that? The ambulance is coming. You're going to be okay."

"Is he bleeding anywhere other than his face?"

"I'm not sure. I don't think he's bleeding anywhere else.

It's hard to see. I just saw him fly over the car and land on the pavement. I had to slam on my brakes to keep from hitting him, too." His hands were trembling as he gripped his phone.

"I understand. Don't move him. Paramedics are on their way. Stay on the line until they arrive and let me know if anything changes."

"Okay." The sound of the first siren increased in volume and was joined by another in a cacophony punctuated by horn blasts. Blue and red flashing lights advanced rapidly.

The 911 dispatcher spoke. "Fire Rescue, may I interrupt?"

"Go ahead."

"The police are almost there, sir. Did you see the vehicle that hit the bike?"

"All I saw were the taillights. The car stopped for a few seconds, then it took off."

"Heading west on 434?"

"Yes. I'm sorry. I wish I'd gotten a better look."

The loudest siren silenced as a police car rolled to a stop.

"Okay, sir. The police are there. I'm going to let you go now so you can speak with the officer."

Samantha Lawrence pressed the garage door button from her car. As the door slowly rose, the bright interior light came on. She winced as the illumination spilled out onto the dark driveway and the damaged front of her red BMW. She pulled in and pressed the button again. The noise of rollers seemed louder than they'd ever been before.

Close. Close. Before anyone hears and sees me.

The door finally closed. She shoved the gear shift into park and fumbled past the fabric from the deployed airbag to reach the ignition and turn off the engine. For a moment, she leaned back against the headrest and closed her eyes, seeking an escape that didn't come. The vision of the bicycle, the rider flying into the air and hitting her windshield, and the airbag exploding in her face flashed in front of her.

She pushed the airbag up over the steering wheel and got out of the car. Surprised by how steady she was, she entered the house, turned off the alarm, and flicked off the garage light. She knew it would have gone off by itself in a few minutes, but she didn't want to chance anyone noticing it through the panes at the top of the garage door.

As she walked into the dark kitchen, her steadiness evaporated. Waves of fear washed over her.

What have I done?

Her knees buckled and she sank to the floor.

~

The hours before dawn were Joy Shepherd's favorite time of day. With most of the world still sleeping, she savored the stillness, the fragrance of the cool night air, and the promise of a sun soon to rise on a new day.

One of the many things she loved about owning and managing Joyful Cup Coffee & Tea was getting to the store early, having that time to herself as she brewed those first pots of coffee before the conversations began to hum and the dishes began to clatter. Her first wave of customers were the hurried commuters who stopped on their way to work to grab a muffin and a to-go cup of their favorite morning beverage. Later on, the customers would be more leisurely. Some would enjoy their coffee and pastries in the shop with friends. Others used the comfortable space and free Wi-Fi to read, work, or hold business meetings. Customers included students, working people, stay-at-home parents, and retirees. Joy considered her regulars to be extended family. She kept track of them and had forged relationships that extended beyond the walls of her store.

Driving to work in the dark, Joy approached State Road 434 from a side street. Glancing to her left, she saw the red and blue flashing lights of emergency vehicles and heard the noise of a helicopter overhead. Police? Medical? Media? She couldn't tell as it flew off into a night sky that would soon begin to lighten.

She said a prayer as she turned right to head toward her shop, glancing in her rearview mirror at the fading flashing lights. What had happened? She would find out soon enough.

The chill she felt had nothing to do with the outside temperature.

~

Toby's wet nose nuzzled Heather Wyland's face. As she reached to gently push him away, she realized light was streaming into the bedroom. She glanced at the clock—almost eight. Why had Kevin allowed her to sleep so late? Throwing back the covers, she made her way to the bathroom, the big black dog following closely.

"Where's your daddy?" She knew Kevin had gone out early for a ride, something he did four or five days a week. He'd ride his bicycle twenty miles in the dark, then come home, take Toby out, and shower before waking her. But the bathroom bore no evidence of his routine this morning and Toby's urgent prancing indicated he hadn't been out yet. "Okay, boy. Hold on. Let me get my robe."

Unease gnawed at her as she led Toby to the back door and opened it. The dog bounded into the small fenced yard, energized by the cool morning air. Heather turned and strode barefoot through the living room into the kitchen. No sign of Kevin. She checked the garage. His bike wasn't in its place. He should have returned more than two hours ago. Her stomach churned. Where could he be? Telling herself not to panic, she rushed to their home office where they kept their cell phones at night. Kevin's phone was on the desk, still plugged into the charger. In spite of her urging him to take his phone with him on his rides, he didn't bother unless he was planning to stop somewhere. The conversation they'd had countless times played in her head.

"Who am I going to call at that hour of the morning?" he'd ask.

"You never know," she'd answer. "There might be an emergency."

"Everyone is tethered to their phones. Someone else can make the call," he'd say, kissing her on the nose. "Besides, nothing is going to happen. Don't worry."

She was worried. And she couldn't call him.

She pressed her fingertips to her temples. Should she call

the police? Was there anything they could do?

She and Kevin were casually acquainted with a few of the officers who patrolled the area. The police department maintained a strong relationship with local merchants, and officers would regularly stop in their pet supply store just to check on things. Though Winter Springs was geographically large and growing in population, it was in many ways a small town. People knew each other. The police chief even had his own social media accounts and was always quick to answer questions from citizens.

She picked up her phone and scrolled through her contact list to the police department's non-emergency number. Taking a deep breath, she tapped the call button on her screen.

"Winter Springs Police Department. How may I help you?" The woman's voice was warm yet professional.

"I'm not sure. My husband went out for a bike ride early this morning. He should have been back a couple of hours ago."

"Your name, please?"

"Heather Wyland."

"May I have your husband's name and description?"

"His name is Kevin Wyland. He's six-one, light brown hair."

"Any distinguishing marks? Tattoos? Piercings?"

"He has an eagle on his left shoulder."

"Okay, Mrs. Wyland. There was an accident on 434 this morning." Heather's heart raced as the woman continued, "We've been issuing traffic alerts, and I know the road is clear now, but I don't have any details on the people involved. I'm going to pass this information on to the investigating officer. May I have your address and phone number?"

Heather rattled off the information and listened impatiently as the woman confirmed it. "Will you get back to me?"

"Yes, ma'am. Someone will call you."

"When?"

"As soon as we know something."

"Should I go look for him? I know where he usually rides."

"No, ma'am. Please don't do that. Stay home and let us do our job."

Heather disconnected the call and reminded herself to breathe.

Please, God, let him be okay.

Toby pawed at the back door. She let him in and watched as he trotted to his food dish. At least something about this morning was normal.

The rich aroma of freshly-brewed coffee filled the air at Joyful Cup. It was the usual weekday crowd, but not the usual weekday chatter. This morning most of the conversation was focused on the hit-and-run crash just a few miles down the road from Town Center. The four-lane divided highway had been shut down in both directions to allow the medical helicopter to land and airlift the victim to the trauma center. Many of Joy's customers had received text and email alerts to avoid the area. Others had seen and contributed to social media discussions, offering prayers for the unidentified victim and hoping the driver would be found and punished.

Wearing her usual jeans and Joyful Cup t-shirt with her long red hair bound in a neat braid, Joy stayed busy behind the counter, filling orders, keeping the line moving while still engaging personally with each customer. Molly, the young barista who had worked with her for two years, mirrored Joy's friendliness and efficiency.

Joy took advantage of a brief lull in customer traffic to do some cleanup in the dining area before the next wave of customers. The eclectic furnishings matched her own taste and the needs of her varied clientele: bistro tables along the large front window, sturdy square tables in the center of the room that could be easily rearranged to accommodate working groups of various sizes, and overstuffed chairs and loveseats flanked by end tables at the back. In the shop, Joy served food and beverages using an assortment of mugs, glasses, and plates that she had purchased from garage sales and thrift shops. It was one of her trademarks. Disposable materials were only used for to-go items.

Joy cleared and wiped the empty tables, changed out the bin of dirty dishes on the stand near the door, and restocked the small supply bar near the counter with stirrers, napkins, creamers, and sweeteners. She checked the glass front of the food display cases for fingerprints—they were surprisingly clean this morning—then headed back behind the counter.

"Rough morning?" Joy offered a sympathetic smile to the next customer in line, a police sergeant who came in almost every day.

"Yeah, and it's not over. Regular coffee to go, please." Sergeant Grant's clipped words matched the weary expression on his face.

Joy deftly slipped a paper cup into a cardboard sleeve, filled it with steaming coffee, and snapped on a plastic lid. "Everyone's wondering who got hit this morning."

"Don't know. He didn't have any ID. Hoping he'll regain consciousness."

His shoulder radio squawked and he turned his head to speak quietly into it. Turning back to Joy, he put some bills on the counter and reached for his coffee. "Sounds like somebody is looking for him. See you later."

After she fed Toby, Heather decided to get dressed while she waited for the police to call her back. Florida weather in March meant cool nights and mild days, so she tugged on a pair of jeans and a long-sleeved cotton top then pulled her dark brown hair into a pony tail. She considered putting on makeup, but her hands were too unsteady. Besides, she didn't care what she looked like.

Lord, I need to know where Kevin is and that he's okay.

Toby followed her as she paced around the house. "Good boy." She stroked his head with one hand and clutched her phone with the other. "You want to know what's going on, don't you? So do I."

She prayed, hoping God would hear and understand her disjointed, frantic pleas. She told herself that just because there had been an accident on the route he usually rode, it didn't mean that Kevin was involved. But if he wasn't involved, where was he? He was one of the most reliable people she had ever known. For him not to come home in time to get their store open was totally out of character, something he would never do.

The store! On weekdays, Heather and Kevin opened the store together at nine o'clock. They had one full-time employee who came in at noon. It was already almost nine. Maybe Emily could come in early so the store wouldn't open too much past its scheduled time. The two part-time employees couldn't because they didn't have keys. Heather quickly tapped out a text.

Can you open the store as soon as possible? Will explain later.

Back to waiting and wondering. Should she call the police again? No, they said they'd call her back. But what if the person who took her call hadn't been able to reach the investigating officer?

She almost dropped her phone when it chimed. A text from Emily.

Sure. I'll be there in about an hour.

As Heather replied with a simple thanks, Toby's ears perked

up. With a soft "woof," he trotted to the front door, taking his usual protective place just before the doorbell rang.

Through the living room window, Heather saw a police car in front of the house. Her stomach knotted. She opened the door slightly. Unable to speak, she stared at the police sergeant standing on her porch.

"Mrs. Wyland? Heather Wyland?"

She nodded.

"I'm Sergeant Grant with the Winter Springs Police Department. I'm here about your husband, Kevin Wyland. He was involved in an accident this morning. He's in the hospital."

"Accident?" It was the only word she could manage.

"May I come in?"

Heather stepped back, opening the door the rest of the way as she clutched Toby's collar. "Yes. Please. Is he okay?"

"I don't know the severity of his injuries. He was hit by a car while riding his bicycle. He's been airlifted to the trauma center in Orlando."

Airlifted. Trauma. The words caused the knot in her stomach to tighten. "I need to see him."

"Of course. I'll take you. Is anyone else here with you?"

"No."

"Let's get your house locked up. I'll tell you more on the way."

Pain consumed Kevin's entire body. He had never felt anything like this before. Lying on a hard surface with his neck in a brace, he couldn't move. All he could see was the brightly-lit ceiling. There had been a flurry of activity, of X-rays and scans, of doctors, nurses, and technicians doing things, asking him questions, snapping instructions to each other. Now the trauma room was quiet. He wasn't sure if anyone else was still there.

Someone had placed a call button by his hand and told him what to do if he needed anything.

He needed Heather. He needed to breathe. He needed someone to do something about the pain that worsened with every breath he tried to take. He needed to know he was going to be okay.

He did his best to focus, to organize what he knew.

He remembered being on his bike, riding as hard as he could, his legs pumping the pedals, his grip firm on the handlebars.

Then confusion.

A voice saying, "Dude, stay with me. The ambulance is coming."

Lots of noise and lights.

He must have lost consciousness because the next thing he remembered was a different voice saying, "Don't try to move, buddy. You were hit by a car. You're on a helicopter and we're on the way to the hospital. Can you tell me your name?" He tried, but he couldn't speak. "That's okay, we're almost there."

Noises faded in and out. A sense of motion as he was wheeled from the landing pad into the building. Pain. And people—lots of people. Talking to each other, occasionally asking him a question he couldn't answer, telling him to be still while they did a CT scan. Finally someone said, "Check his left shoulder for a tattoo," then a nurse leaned over him and asked, "Is your name Kevin Wyland?"

He couldn't move his head but he found the breath to answer weakly. "Yes."

"Okay, don't try to talk. The police are notifying your wife and she'll be here soon."

He wanted to smile, but instead felt a tear slipping from the corner of his eye.

He heard a little more conversation among the medical team, and then no more voices, only the soft beeping of monitors.

How long ago had that been? There was no sense of time in this bright, sterile room.

He knew he should pray. But he couldn't.

"I've never been in a police car before." It was the only thing Heather could think of to say as she fastened her seatbelt.

"That's a good thing." Sergeant Grant's expression was kind. "Try to relax, Mrs. Wyland."

"What happened to Kevin?"

"He was hit from behind by a car while he was riding on 434 about five o'clock this morning. A witness called 911. EMS responded within a few minutes. They determined he needed to be airlifted to the trauma center."

Heather processed the sergeant's dispassionate words.

"Did you speak to him?"

"No. I didn't get the initial call. By the time I got there, he was already on the helicopter. I understand he was semi-conscious, but he didn't say anything. That's not unusual. He was probably in shock. But he didn't have any identification."

"I know." Heather sighed. "He never takes his phone, either. He won't take anything that isn't absolutely necessary. He says he doesn't want anything that will slow him down." Heather wondered if Sergeant Grant would comment on that. He didn't.

"When we got your call, we were able to match up the description you gave us with what we had from the scene. We called the hospital and confirmed his identity."

"But you don't know anything about his condition?"

"Nothing definite."

"Can you tell me—" She stopped. "I'm sorry. I guess I'm trying to get you to tell me that he's going to be okay."

"I'm sorry, Mrs. Wyland. I can't say that." Sergeant Grant hesitated. "I can tell you this much: He bounced over the car, hit the windshield, and landed on the pavement. That's a lot of trauma. He was wearing a helmet but you still need to prepare yourself for him to have some serious injuries."

"And the driver?"

"Hit and run. The witness didn't get a good description, but we were able to collect some evidence at the scene."

"Was there only one witness?"

"Yes. A man on his way to work. He saw it happen and stopped. Not much traffic at that hour."

Heather wanted to reply but couldn't think of anything to say. They rode in silence. After a while, Heather pulled her gaze from the window and looked around the interior of the car, focusing on the paper cup in the holder on the console.

"Coffee from Joyful Cup?" It was trivial, but right now she needed something trivial to distract her from thoughts of what might be waiting for her at the hospital.

"That's where I was when your call came in."

"Our shop is just a few doors down in Town Center." She named the planned suburban "downtown" area of stores, offices, and restaurants. "We've known Joy since we opened it."

"I'm one of Joy's regulars. What's your store?"

"Wyland's Pet Food and Supplies. We sell—obviously—pet food, the high quality brands that grocery stores don't carry, supplies, gifts. Mostly for dogs and cats, but we carry a few items for other domestic pets." She automatically gave the response that had become standard when anyone asked about their business.

"Sounds like a fun business to be in."

"It is." Heather's gaze returned to the window. She focused on landmarks that told her they had arrived at the massive hospital complex. "Thank you for driving me."

"You're welcome. We don't want you driving yourself under circumstances like these." He pulled into a reserved parking area. "Come on. Let's go find your husband."

Kevin wondered how much longer he would have to lie motionless on this hard surface, how much longer it would be before they gave him something for the pain, how much longer it would be before Heather got there. Then he heard the voice of the nurse who had identified him earlier. "Good news, Mr. Wyland, your wife is here."

"Kevin!"

A second after he heard her voice, he felt her hands on his arm. "You're here," he whispered. "Let me see you, Sunshine."

Heather drew a breath and the nurse spoke. "Mrs. Wyland, you'll need to lean over him so he can see you. He can't turn his head right now. We can't take the brace off until we get the CT back, but it shouldn't be much longer."

"Thank you." As she responded to the nurse, Heather stretched to move into Kevin's line of vision. "I'm here. How do you feel?"

"Everything hurts. But it's better now that you're here." He blinked his eyes a few times to help him focus on Heather's face.

"I was so scared."

"I know. I'm sorry." His voice was getting stronger, but it was still a struggle to speak. "Are you okay?"

"I'm fine. But you—you've got dried blood on your face, and you're swollen. I think your nose is broken."

"Maybe that's why it's so hard to breathe."

The nurse patted his shoulder. "Try to relax, Mr. Wyland. Once we get the scans back, we'll be able to get you cleaned up and make you more comfortable. I'll check back in a little while, but if you need anything, use the call button."

Kevin heard rustling as the nurse left the room. "Do you know what happened?"

"Shush. Don't talk." Heather gently touched his lips with her index finger. "Toby woke me up when you didn't come home. I called the police and they brought me here. You can't see him, but Sergeant Grant is here."

As Heather looked over her shoulder, a male voice spoke. "Mr. Wyland, I'm Josh Grant. I've been assigned to investigate your case."

"Where's my bike?"

Sergeant Grant chuckled. "That's the most common question I get from the rider in a car-versus-bike crash. Right now, your bike is in the trunk of my car. I picked it up at the scene this morning. We'll keep it for a while to process it for evidence, then you can have it back."

"How is it?"

"In worse shape than you. Probably not repairable." The sergeant chuckled again. "But you may still want to keep it. Mrs.

Wyland, before I leave, is there anyone I can call for you? Family? A friend?"

"Could you call our pastor? I've got his number in my phone." Heather pulled her hands away so she could get to her phone. Kevin resisted the urge to try to grab her arm. "We don't have family here."

"I'll call him before I leave the hospital. Is there anything else I can do for you?"

As Kevin was trying to think of what else a police officer could possibly do for them, Heather spoke. "I don't know how this works, but can you not release Kevin's name yet? Give us a chance to find out what's going on with his injuries and talk to our families first."

The sergeant agreed, promising to check back later. As he left, Heather turned back to Kevin. "We don't want your mom or your sister finding out about this from someone else, and I don't want to call them until we know what's going on."

"That's my wife, always thinking. You're so smart."

"Smart enough to marry you, anyway." She leaned over to gently kiss his cheek. "It's going to be okay. You're going to be fine."

Though she was smiling, he could see the worry in her eyes. He wasn't sure if she was trying to reassure him or herself.

How long had she been on the kitchen floor? Samantha wasn't sure. It had been dark when she came in. It was daylight now—it had been for a while. She should get up and do something. But what?

What do you do after you hit a bicyclist and drive away?

As she struggled to her feet, she heard a plaintive meow. The white and gray cat began circling her legs, demanding to be fed. Samantha forced herself through the motions of opening a can of food, filling a dish, and putting it on the floor. Such an ordinary thing to do, something she did every morning. Even this morning. This horrible morning.

She leaned against the kitchen counter. How could she have done what she did? And what should she do now?

Last night had been so normal. She and her friend Amber had gone out as they often did on Wednesdays—they called it their hump day break. So they didn't have to worry about parking or driving home after they'd been drinking, they used a ride-sharing service to get from Amber's apartment, where Samantha had left her car, to the Ivanhoe Village district of Orlando. It was almost two in the morning when the SafeRide driver dropped them back off Amber's.

Samantha decided to get a few hours of sleep on Amber's couch before heading home. When her alarm sounded at five, she quickly silenced it, splashed some water on her face, then quietly let herself out, trying not to disturb her friend. She would go home, shower, feed the cat, and be at school in time for her eight o'clock class. At that hour, few other cars were on the road. She was just a couple of miles from her house when her phone buzzed with a text from Amber.

Got me a new pair of sunglasses.

Samantha laughed to herself. She was always leaving her sunglasses somewhere. That's why she kept spares in various places the way her grandmother had done with reading glasses.

Glancing at her phone, her thumb moved quickly over the screen as she replied.

No way. Get your own.

Then she looked up from her phone and saw the bike.

And felt the impact.

The rider struck her windshield. The airbag exploded in her face. For a few seconds, she couldn't see, couldn't breathe. Then the airbag deflated into a pile of fabric on her lap and a distinct chemical odor permeated her car. She didn't remember braking, but she must have because her car was stopped. She saw headlights in the rearview mirror.

She pressed her foot on the accelerator and sped away.

Now here she was, standing in the kitchen, watching the cat eat, trying to figure out what to do.

Heather clung to Kevin's hand as the doctor and his entourage walked away. Though her body was still, her emotions were on a roller coaster. Fear, relief, anxiety, panic, and hope fought for control. She managed a weak smile.

"At least we know what we're dealing with now."

Kevin was silent, staring at the ceiling. Heather knew he was processing everything the doctor had said. So was she.

She wished she'd been able to take notes as the doctor rapidly listed Kevin's injuries and treatment plan. A closed head injury consisting of a subdural hematoma and an intracranial hemorrhage sounded frightening, but the doctor assured Kevin and Heather that they were small and should heal without treatment. The fractured pelvis and broken ribs would take much longer. The broken nose and facial lacerations weren't serious. But the spinal fracture would require surgery. Kevin would be moved to Intensive Care where he would be monitored for the rest of the day and, barring any complications, undergo surgery tomorrow.

The doctor said Kevin was lucky. Though his injuries were serious, they could have been much worse and he would recover.

It was going to be a long journey neither one of them had ever thought about taking.

Realizing that she couldn't just stand in the kitchen forever,

Samantha finally went upstairs and showered. Maybe if she could wash away the smell of the air bag chemicals she would be able to think clearly, to formulate a plan and figure out what she should do.

Dealing with something this major by herself was a new experience. At 22, Samantha had never been completely on her own. Though she'd taken a year off between high school and college, she'd stayed at home with her parents in Toledo. When she was ready to go to college, she looked for a school that would keep her close to family but let her be independent.

A key reason the University of Central Florida was one of her top college choices was that her grandmother lived nearby in Winter Springs. The three-bedroom townhouse had plenty of room for Samantha, who could attend classes and assist Gram with things she could no longer manage on her own. The two were best friends. Gram observed more than once that the arrangement was ideal because Samantha was learning to be independent while helping her grandmother stay independent. But a few months ago, Gram had a massive stroke and died.

Samantha's mother was the primary beneficiary of Gram's estate, which included the townhouse, furnishings, a car, some modest investments, and Lucy, the cat. The family decided Samantha would continue to live in the house while the estate was being settled and possibly even until she finished school.

Out of the shower, Samantha inspected herself in the mirror. Wide hazel eyes stared back at her. As usual, her shoulder-length blonde hair framed her face with damp curls. Stress had drained the natural color from her complexion. There was a red mark on her left cheek, probably the beginning of a bruise from the airbag, but no other outward sign that she had hit someone, possibly killed him, and driven away. And for the first time, she was glad her beloved grandmother was dead.

With amazing efficiency, the ICU team got Kevin settled in his room and hooked up to an assortment of monitors. A nurse gently sponged the last of the dried blood off of his face and treated the abrasions on his hands and legs. Another nurse showed Heather the bag containing Kevin's things—the clothes they had cut off him, his helmet, a shoe—and gave what amounted to an orientation, pointing out call buttons, light switches, and vending machines. Heather was welcome to sleep on the sofa in Kevin's room and the hospital would provide a pillow and linens. And then Heather and Kevin were alone to face a day of waiting together.

"Want me to turn on the TV?" Heather smiled when Kevin's response was a negative grunt. He didn't like watching television and, obviously, being in the hospital wasn't going to change that. She pulled a chair next to the bed and took Kevin's hand.

"Sergeant Grant seems like a nice guy. He drove me here so I didn't have to drive myself. I didn't know the police would do that." She knew she was on the verge of babbling, saying anything that wasn't a question because she didn't want Kevin to talk but felt a need to fill the silence. "He's a regular customer at Joyful Cup. I told him about our store, but I don't know if he has any pets. I texted Emily and she said she could come in early to get the store open."

"Good. She gets a bonus for this." His voice was barely above a whisper.

"I should call her and let her know what's going on."

Kevin's grip on Heather's hand tightened. "Not yet. Stay."

"I'm not going anywhere." Heather suspected a combination of shock and pain medication was making Kevin cling to her. And that was okay, because she wanted to cling to him. Phone calls could wait.

~

Samantha couldn't put it off any longer. She needed to see how badly her car was damaged.

The only windows in the garage were at the top of the door, so it was dim even in the middle of the day. She flipped the light switch, took a few steps toward her car, and hit her head on the seat of her bicycle, which was hanging from the ceiling. She froze and squeezed her eyes shut, fighting the sudden tears that were totally out of proportion to the pain from the mild bump. She'd ridden that bike on countless weekend outings with her friends. Would she ever feel safe on it again?

She couldn't think about that now. After a few deep breaths, she was ready to inspect the front of her red BMW 328i. The car was a hand-me-down from her mother, who wanted to be sure she had something safe and reliable to drive while she was in college. The irony of that wasn't lost on Samantha as she examined the broken headlight, scratches on the front bumper, dents and scrapes on the hood, and broken windshield. All this damage and she was fine except for a small bruise on her cheek. But how was the bicyclist she'd hit?

She pushed the thought of the victim from her mind and focused on what to do about her car. Though it was technically drivable, Samantha knew she couldn't go anywhere in it in that condition. The broken windshield and deployed airbag were dangerous. And someone would surely ask how the damage happened. At least for now, the car needed to stay hidden in the garage.

She'd already missed her morning classes, so she could stay home the rest of the day. She didn't have any classes the next day, Friday, and if anyone wanted to hang out over the weekend, she'd just beg off and say she was busy with schoolwork. If she needed anything, she could walk to Town Center. That was something she did regularly, anyway, so no one would think it was unusual. Since Gram died, she would often take her laptop to Joyful Cup and drink coffee while she studied or worked on projects. It was better than being alone in the house. She was a regular customer at several of the other stores as well—the hair salon, the supermarket, the Vietnamese restaurant, the pet supply store that carried the special cat food Gram had always bought for Lucy.

If she hadn't figured out anything else before Monday when she had to go back to school, she would just drive Gram's car. If anyone asked, she could say she was just driving it because it had been parked for months.

She turned out the light and went back in the house, trying not to think about how easily she had come up with the lies and excuses.

Heather spent the night dozing fitfully on the sofa in Kevin's hospital room. Nurses had been in and out, monitoring Kevin and offering support to Heather. Though they obviously tried to be as quiet as possible, the activity made sound sleep impossible.

As the early light of dawn came through the window, sounds of the hospital's morning routines filtered in from the hallway—the nursing staff preparing for shift change, housekeepers pushing carts of linens and cleaning supplies, food service workers rattling trays. Heather stood up and stretched, first reaching up then bending over and rolling up to ease the tension in her spine.

"Wish I could do that." Kevin's voice was still weak, but stronger than it had been yesterday.

"I didn't mean to wake you." Heather moved to the side of the bed and took Kevin's hand.

"We're in the hospital. No sleeping allowed."

"That's what everyone says."

A tap at the door was followed by, "Okay if I come in?"

"Emily!" Heather was surprised to see their employee. "Of course, come in."

"I thought you could use some things." Emily held out a small gift bag. "There's a toothbrush, toothpaste, some lotion, and some snacks."

"Snacks?" The mention of food got Kevin's attention.

"Hey, boss. You look like you've been in a fight."

"Thanks. I feel like it, too. What kind of snacks?"

Heather checked out the contents of the bag. "The kind you can't eat right now." She turned to Emily. "The doctor should be in soon to let us know what time he's scheduled for surgery. That's why he can't have anything to eat or drink."

"But *you* need to eat. We don't need another patient." Emily was always practical—one of the characteristics that Heather and Kevin appreciated about her. "I'll get the store open this morning. Jacob and Nicole will come in later." She referred to the two part-time employees who were part of the store's small team. "I'll take a couple of hours off this afternoon and go back to close. It's all under control—you don't need to worry about it."

"Thank you."

"What else can I do? Where's Toby?"

"Our next door neighbor is taking care of him."

"Want me to pick him up and let him spend the day in the store?"

Heather and Kevin usually took Toby to work with them. He was the store's official greeter. "That would be wonderful. Our neighbor is just coming over to take him out and feed him. He's not used to being left alone."

"I know. And we miss him at the store. Look, I'll go get him now and take him home with me tonight. He'll be fine."

"Thanks. I'll give you the garage door code so you can get in. And I'll let our neighbor know you're coming."

"One more thing. Is it okay to let people know what happened? I mean, everyone knows there was a hit-and-run yesterday morning, but no one knows it was Kevin."

"Thanks for not saying anything." Heather had asked Emily to not tell anyone why she and Kevin were not in the store yesterday so she could notify family members before Kevin's identity got out on the news and social media. "We called Kevin's mom and sister last night. It's okay to tell people now. But only people you see—no posting on social media. And ask them not to call or visit."

"Understood. Let me know when you find out about the surgery. I want to be praying."

For the first time since Sergeant Grant knocked on her door twenty-four hours ago, hot tears stung Heather's eyes.

"Good morning. What brings you out this early?" Joy was wiping tables when Emily walked into her shop. Though Emily was a regular Joyful Cup customer, she rarely came in before lunch.

"I'm opening the store for Kevin and Heather, and I need caffeine."

"You've come to the right place. Molly will get you fixed up." Joy picked up a used coffee stirrer off the floor. "Why the new schedule?"

"You know the hit-and-run yesterday? That was Kevin. He was on his bike and a car hit him from behind."

"Oh, no!" It was as much a plea as an exclamation. "How is he?"

"Hurt pretty bad. I stopped by the hospital this morning. He was awake and talking, but he's supposed to have surgery on his spine today."

"And Heather?" Joy twisted the stirrer she was holding.

"Exhausted. She's putting on a brave face, but I know she's worried. She spent the night at the hospital. She didn't want to leave him."

"That's understandable." Joy sighed deeply. "I'm so sorry to hear this. What can I do?"

"Nothing I can think of. They don't want any visitors. I've got Toby, and I don't know that there's anything else they need at this point."

"Keep me posted. And let me know if *you* need anything. Now, let's get you some coffee." With her arm across Emily's shoulders, Joy guided her to the counter and spoke to the barista. "Molly, this one's on the house."

Joy brushed aside Emily's protests and returned to her task of wiping tables. As she worked, she recalled the sudden chill she felt when she saw the emergency lights at the crash yesterday morning. And now she understood it.

Samantha had to get out of the house.

She had just spent the longest night of her life. Every time she closed her eyes, she saw the bicycle, heard the horrible thud, and saw the man hit her windshield. Sleep was impossible, so she gave up trying. When she wasn't pacing from room to room, she was searching for local news online, trying to find out what happened to the rider she had hit. All she could find was a few mentions in community social media groups about the road being temporarily closed due to a traffic accident. She considered posting a comment asking for details, then decided it might cast suspicion on her. Surely if he had died that would have made a headline on a local television station's website, so he must have survived. But why couldn't she find out?

Maybe some fresh air and being around people would help. She dressed quickly in a set of the casual shorts and tops she often wore, adding a lightweight hoodie that would keep her comfortable until the day reached its full warmth. The red mark on her cheek had darkened to a purple bruise, still visible under makeup. There wasn't anything else she could do to hide it. If anyone asked about it, she'd come up with some explanation. People got bruises all the time.

Shoving her laptop, wallet, and keys in her backpack, she

headed out on foot. She would spend some time at Joyful Cup. The owner, Joy, knew everybody and would probably be able to answer Samantha's questions—if she could figure out how to ask discretely.

It was a beautiful March morning, sunny and cool. The blistering, humid heat of summer in Florida was still a couple of months away. Samantha walked through her neighborhood without seeing anyone she knew. As she reached the main street, she paused and looked down the road to the east. She couldn't quite see where the accident had occurred, but it wasn't far. Maybe later she'd go to the exact spot and see what was there. But not now.

She crossed the busy street and made her way into Town Center, following her usual route to Joyful Cup. She ordered a latte, settled at one of the bistro tables near the window, opened her laptop, and pulled up some notes for a project she was working on for a mass media class. Then she stared out the window.

"We have iced lattes, you know." Joy smiled and nodded toward Samantha's untouched cup. "You don't have to let it sit there and get cold."

"What? Oh. I know." It took Samantha a few seconds to figure out what Joy meant. She took a sip of her lukewarm drink. "I was just thinking."

Joy pulled out a chair and sat down. "Big project?"

"Not really." This was what Samantha had hoped for—a chance to talk with Joy. And now she didn't know what to say. "I'm just having some trouble getting started."

"When I'm stuck on something, it helps me to take a break from it, come back later when I'm fresh." Joy glanced out the window then returned her gaze to Samantha. "I hope you don't mind me saying so, you look tired."

"I'm okay. I was just up late last night." Samantha wondered if Joy was looking at the bruise on her cheek.

"I'm glad you're not coming down with something. Some nasty bugs are going around."

"No, I'm just short on sleep." How could she bring the conversation around to the accident? "I don't know how you always look so fresh, especially when you get here so early in the morning."

Joy chuckled. "I'm not in college and I don't stay up late. Want me to warm that up for you?" As she rose, she pointed toward Samantha's latte.

"No, thanks." Samantha was searching for something else to say to keep Joy talking when the door opened. A police officer walked in. She felt the blood drain from her face.

"If you're sure." Joy smiled at Samantha, then looked toward the door. "Good morning, Sergeant Grant. I hope you're having a better day than you were yesterday."

The officer smiled warmly at Joy. "It's been quiet. That's always good." Samantha saw his gaze pass over her as he scanned the room. Did he notice how tightly she was gripping the edge of the table?

Joy patted Samantha's shoulder and took a few steps toward the officer. "Can I get you some coffee? And how about a lemon poppy seed muffin?"

Sergeant Grant's smile shifted to a mock grimace. "For every minute I spend in here, I need to spend ten in the gym. But it's worth it." He chose a table near the counter that afforded him a clear view of the door and the window. Thankful that he was sitting close enough for her to hear what he said, Samantha watched surreptitiously as Joy served him coffee in a souvenir mug from Savannah, Georgia and a muffin on a light blue plate.

"Hope you don't mind helping me test a new supplier—a

bakery that just opened down the street. Let me know what you think."

The sergeant inhaled deeply. "Smells delicious. I thought your other suppliers were good."

"They are. But I like having options, and this one is a small business, locally owned. We independents need to stick together." Joy sat down in the chair across from the police officer. "I heard that Kevin Wyland was the hit-and-run victim."

"Yeah." The sergeant sipped his coffee. "His wife woke up yesterday and he wasn't back from his ride. She called and we were able to make the ID."

Kevin Wyland. The name sounded familiar, but Samantha couldn't place it.

"Did you know he and his wife own the pet supply store here in the center?" Joy asked.

Now the name clicked for Samantha. Wyland's Pet Food and Supplies. Of course. Gram bought Lucy's food there, but she always referred to it as simply the cat food store.

"She told me while I was taking her to the hospital. Have you heard how he's doing?" The sergeant took a bite of his muffin. Samantha's mind was racing. If the sergeant had driven the victim's wife to the hospital, it meant he was still alive. He hadn't died from the accident.

Joy's brow furrowed slightly. "One of his employees stopped by this morning. Said he's supposed to have surgery on his spine today."

"I'm not surprised. He was pretty banged up when I saw him. He'll probably recover, but it's going to be a long road."

Samantha was weak with relief. He was alive and he would recover. She hadn't killed him. He hadn't died because she didn't stop.

Gram often spoke fondly of the young couple who owned the pet supply store, talking about how friendly they were, how the man teased her, suggesting that she adopt several more cats so she would have to buy more food and toys. After Gram died, Samantha continued buying Lucy's food there. Once when she was in the store and the owners were there, she introduced herself and told them about Gram's passing. They seemed genuine in their sympathy and from then on appeared to make an extra effort to be kind and compassionate to Samantha. She started to reach for her cup, then dropped her hand back on the table when she realized she was trembling.

She dragged her attention back to the conversation between Joy and Sergeant Grant.

"Any idea who the driver was?" Joy asked.

"Not yet. There was a witness, but he didn't get a tag number. The car was damaged, though. And we have some other evidence."

"Enough to figure out who it was?"

The leather of his duty belt creaked as he leaned back in his seat. "Probably, but it will take months to get the reports back. This is real life, not television. It takes the labs a long time to identify the debris we find at crashes. Our best bet is if the driver takes the car in for repair and the repair shop reports the damage. Or sometimes someone who knows the driver well will report it because the driver told them about it or they saw damage to the car. We'll do a Crimeline reward. People will sell out their mother for money."

"That's so cynical." As Joy said the words aloud, Samantha was thinking the same thing.

"It's true."

"Whatever it takes. A lot of people are hoping you find the guy."

"We'll try, but don't hold your breath. Hit-and-runs are hard to solve."

Samantha realized she was, ironically, holding her breath.

She exhaled slowly. This time, when she reached for her cup, her hand was steady.

~

The minutes dragged by slowly as Kevin and Heather waited for him to be taken to the operating room.

"You should go home. There's nothing you can do here." He squeezed her hand gently.

"I should be here. I'm not leaving you." Heather stood next to the bed, wanting to be as close to Kevin as possible for as long as possible.

"You need a shower."

"Yeah? So do you."

"You need something to eat."

"I've eaten. Stop it, Kevin." Affectionate exasperation was clear in her tone. "I'm not leaving. Maybe later, after you're out of surgery."

He turned his head and stared at the ceiling. "I'm sorry about this."

"Stop that, too. It was an accident. It wasn't your fault. And you're going to be fine." She forced a note of confidence into her voice that she didn't entirely feel.

"I don't like to think of you sitting here alone for hours while I'm in surgery."

"I won't be alone. Pastor Brett is coming by and I think he's lining up people from our small group to take turns sitting with me. I'll probably have more company than I want."

Thanks to Sergeant Grant notifying the pastor of their church, Heather had been spared the task of repeating the story of the crash to multiple friends. The pastor had arrived at the hospital shortly after Kevin was moved to his ICU room the day before. He stayed with Kevin while Heather made essential phone calls—to Kevin's mother in California, to the neighbor so

Toby would be cared for, to Emily so the store would be staffed. Then he told Heather to put down her phone and focus on Kevin while he took care of notifying their church family.

Kevin squeezed her hand again. "Good. Brett's a good guy. He'll take care of you."

"I think you're the one who needs to be taken care of, not me."

"I have doctors."

There was a tap on the door and suddenly the room was bustling with activity—monitors unhooked, IV transferred to a mobile stand, the bed's guardrails raised. It was time.

Heather identified the nurse who seemed to be in charge. "May I go with him?"

"Only to the elevator."

Heather walked next to Kevin as far as she could. At the elevator bank, she leaned over and pressed her lips gently to his. "I love you," she whispered.

"I love you, too. Come here." She understood and shifted her face so he could kiss her nose—his way of telling her not to worry.

The elevator doors opened and Heather stepped back, biting her lip so she wouldn't start crying.

The nurse's expression was sympathetic. "We'll take good care of him, Mrs. Wyland. I promise."

Then the elevator doors whispered shut. She stood there by herself, staring at the silver panels.

Please, God. Please.

Samantha sipped her tepid latte without tasting it. It took all the self-control she could muster to stare at her computer screen and make occasional taps on the keyboard so it wouldn't be obvious that she was eavesdropping on Joy and the police sergeant. Even as she tried to focus on what they were saying, she couldn't help but think about what it meant for her.

She knew the man she'd hit. Not well, but enough to know that he was a popular member of their local community. People were probably angry at the person who had hit him and driven away. But he wasn't dead. He was hurt, he needed surgery, but he didn't die. And he would probably recover. She wasn't a killer. Relief flooded through her as she thought about what else she'd learned.

There was a witness, but he didn't get her tag number. It could take months, if ever, for the police to identify her car. She had plenty of time to figure out how to get it repaired. Was it possible that everything was going to be all right?

She could think about those things later. She needed to listen now because Joy was asking about Heather.

"She seems like a strong person," Sergeant Grant said. "I think most people do better when they find out what happened. It's the not knowing that's so hard. Once she knew there was an accident, she was ready to handle it."

"I'm not surprised. You're right, she's strong. And very

organized and efficient. She's great at making sense out of chaos."

"She's going to have a lot of chaos. I've been doing traffic homicide investigations for years—"

"Traffic homicide?" As Joy said the phrase out loud, Samantha repeated it in her mind. How could there be a homicide investigation if no one died?

"Sorry, it's what we call it. We treat crashes like this the same way we'd treat a crash where someone died. I've seen plenty of car-versus-bike crashes. It's going to take a long time for him to get back to normal—if he ever does. The driver is facing some serious charges and—hey, I'm not a doctor. I think Wyland's going to be okay, but you never know. He could die, he could be paralyzed. So we want all of our investigative ducks in a row." Sergeant Grant took the last bite of his muffin, drained his coffee cup, and stood. He dropped some bills on the table. "That was good. You should keep that flavor in stock."

Joy got to her feet. "Glad you approve. Can I get you a coffee to go?"

"That'd be great. I've got some videos to go through."

"There's video of the crash?"

"No. No cameras in that immediate area. But there are some traffic cams and security cameras from shopping centers that may have caught the car before and after. Might be able to see the damage and track it down." He took his to-go cup and thanked Joy again.

Samantha watched him stride out of the shop. A few moments ago, she was feeling relieved, thinking that everything was going to be okay. Now she wondered if she was going to prison.

There was a family waiting area at the end of the hall, but Heather decided to stay in Kevin's room while he was in surgery. She was right about Pastor Brett notifying their friends—she had a steady stream of people who had obviously coordinated their visits. Only one or two at a time, some with food, others with books or magazines. One friend brought a charger for her phone, another gave her a notebook and pen so she could keep a journal of Kevin's progress. They encouraged her to get out of the room, to at least take short walks on the floor if she didn't want to go further. They offered to run errands, to bring her things she needed. They prayed with her. And when what she needed was silence, they were quiet.

It was late afternoon when the surgeon finally appeared. He looked tired but was smiling when he walked into the room. The surgery had gone well, Kevin was in recovery, and he would be brought back to the room in a few hours. Heather watched the doctor's mouth move with additional details, but she didn't hear them. They didn't matter, anyway. All that mattered was that Kevin was okay.

She relaxed and let the tears flow.

After several minutes of deep breathing, Samantha closed her laptop and put it in her backpack, hoping no one would notice how much she was trembling. As she stood, Joy spoke from behind the counter.

"Finished already? Or did you decide to take my advice and take a break?"

Samantha had to clear her throat twice to get the words out. "Taking your advice." Shrugging into her backpack, she arranged her expression into what she hoped was a smile, waved weakly, and left the shop.

She had planned to pick up a few things at Publix, the grocery store in Town Center, but that could wait. She needed to get home where she had privacy, where no one could look over her shoulder and see what she was researching. This time, as she crossed the street, she avoided looking toward the crash site, but studied the buildings, wondering where the surveillance cameras were.

At home, she quickly unpacked her computer, settled at her desk, and began typing various phrases in the search box. *Hit and run. Leaving the scene of an accident. How are hit and run accidents investigated? Penalties for hit and run. Hit and run prosecution.*

After several hours of reading, she sat back and tried to digest what she had learned. The police had more investigative resources than she had imagined. While a hit-and-run with only a small amount of property damage would be a low priority in terms of investigation and prosecution, one that involved serious bodily injury would get more attention. Though it wasn't unusual for hit-and-run drivers to get away with their crime, many were caught and prosecuted—sometimes weeks or months or even years later. If she were caught, she faced up to five years in prison if Kevin survived and up to thirty years if he died.

But to arrest her, the police would need evidence. What evidence did they have?

There was a witness but he didn't get her license tag number. Did he get a look at her car? At her?

There was no video of the actual crash, but they may be able to match up her car to other videos. Could they prove she was driving?

When she examined the damage to her car, she hadn't seen any blood—but there could have been traces of blood not visible in the dim garage light. And there might be paint or other evidence from the impact with the bicycle. Could she wash that off? She would have to try.

Biting her lip, she closed her browser windows and cleared her search history, then scoffed at herself. How likely was it that the police would ever check her computer? All they needed to arrest her was the evidence from her car and proof that she was driving. She had to make sure they wouldn't find that.

In the kitchen, she filled a bucket with soapy water and headed to the garage. The cat followed her. To avoid being seen, she had to leave the garage door closed as she worked, which made rinsing away the evidence challenging. She scrubbed the dented hood and the area around the broken headlight lens over and over. Finally she stopped, wiped her forehead, and looked at the cat. "I feel like Lady Macbeth. 'Out damned spot!' But I'm not sleepwalking, am I, Lucy? I'm just talking to a cat. I'm not sure which is crazier."

This wasn't going to work. Even if she could clean the car, even if she could replace the headlight lens herself, how was she going to explain the broken windshield, dents on the hood, and deployed airbag?

∽

When Kevin opened his eyes, the first thing he saw was Heather leaning over the bed with a slight smile on her face.

"Hey," she said softly. "How do you feel?"

"Thirsty." He was hoarse. "Where?" He looked around, trying to figure out where he was.

"Don't try to talk. Drink." She held a straw to his lips. "You're in post-op. The surgery went well. The doctor said it was textbook perfect. They'll take you back up to your room a little later."

After several sips of water, he turned his head slightly to let her know he'd had enough. "Can I walk?"

"Tomorrow. They're going to get you out of bed tomorrow."

"And go home?"

"One step at a time. It's going to be at least a week, maybe longer."

"I need to get back to the store." The confusion was clearing.

"You need to concentrate on healing. The store is fine. Emily's got it under control with Jacob and Nicole."

"But ..." He paused, trying to remember. "Today's Friday, right?"

"Right."

"We've got adoptions tomorrow." He referred to the rescue pet adoption event they held once a month. A local rescue group would set up cages and pens of dogs and cats on the sidewalk. In addition to finding homes for the animals, it always generated extra business for them because people would come inside to purchase food and other supplies for their new pets. The adoption events were always all hands on deck and everyone stayed busy.

"I talked with Emily about that. She didn't want to cancel. She says she and Jacob and Nicole will be able to handle it. And Toby will be there with them."

He smiled. "That's right. Emily's got Toby."

"And she's spoiling him rotten." Heather stroked Kevin's cheek. "I'll go by the store tomorrow and give you a full report."

Mentally shaking off the remainder of the anesthesia-induced fog, he sighed in frustration. "Any news from the police? Have they caught the guy?"

"I haven't heard anything. I'll call Sergeant Grant tomorrow."

"You should go home. Get some rest."

"We've already had this conversation. I'm staying. I'll go home in the morning."

"But not for long." He was torn. He wanted her to be comfortable but he didn't want her to leave him.

"No, not for long. Just long enough to shower and check on the store."

"Okay." It was a whisper as his eyes closed and he dozed off.

Saturday morning customers at Joyful Cup were dominated by weekend athletes stopping in for coffee or a sports drink, a light snack, and the chance to recap their runs, rides, and games. They were nosier and sweatier than the weekday customers, but Joy and her crew were always ready for them.

This morning there was a somber note as many of the cyclists talked about what happened to Kevin. Word had gotten around about the crash and his surgery, but no one knew about his prognosis. Speculation was rampant. Would he recover? Be disabled? What sort of help would he need? Would the driver be caught?

Joy spent most of her time circulating in the dining area where she could chat with customers as she picked up dirty dishes and trash, wiped tables and chairs, and maintained as much order as was possible. Her staff could handle the counter, calling on her when necessary. She did her best to quell some of the more outrageous rumors and shared some of what Sergeant Grant had told her about how the investigation would proceed.

The crowd had begun to thin when Heather came in. Joy immediately went to her, enveloping her in a protective hug. "It's good to see you. How are you? How's Kevin? And what are you doing here?"

"I'm fine. Tired, but fine. Kevin's okay. He's worried about the store. So I'm here to get coffee and goodies for everybody and check on things before I head back to the hospital."

"Emily came by yesterday. She said he was having surgery on his spine."

"Yes, and that went well. They got him out of bed for a short walk this morning. He has to use a walker, but he's up. The doctors say his other injuries will heal on their own, with time. And he's feeling well enough to be obsessing about the store, so that's good, right?"

Joy gave her another gentle squeeze and stepped back. "It sounds good to me. And it gives him something to think about besides the accident."

"Actually, I don't think either one of us has thought too much about the accident itself. Well, Kevin's wondering about the investigation. He wants the driver caught. I've been concentrating on him and taking care of things that can't wait. We're both trying to understand his injuries and what it's going to take for him to recover."

"And that's what you need to be focusing on right now. How many coffees do you need?"

"Four, please. I've got three people working in the store and I want one for myself."

Joy gave quick instructions to the barista and then began filling a box with muffins and other baked goods. When the order was ready, Joy refused to let Heather pay. "Let me do this. It's my way of helping. Come on, let me carry that. I'll walk with you."

"Thank you." Once outside, they could hear dogs barking. The adoption event was audibly underway. As they walked toward the noise, Heather continued talking. "People are being so good. Friends were at the hospital yesterday, taking turns sitting with me while Kevin was in surgery. And our pastor was at the hospital early this morning. He drove me home because I didn't have my car. Did you know the police came to notify me and drove me to the hospital?"

"Sergeant Grant was in Joyful Cup getting coffee when he got the word that you had called the police about Kevin."

"So that's why he had one of your cups in his car. Small world."

"He's a good cop. I've known him for years. He's working hard on the investigation. Watch that." Joy pointed to a puddle on the sidewalk that had probably been left by one of the yelping puppies. "You should know that some of Kevin's riding friends were in the shop this morning. They're going to set up a HelpNow account so that people can donate to help you with expenses."

Joy wasn't surprised that Heather didn't reply. It would be difficult for people as independent as the Wylands to accept anything they perceived as charity. The two women stepped past the crates and pens of lively animals and entered the store, where Heather was greeted enthusiastically by Toby, then by Emily, Jacob, and Nicole.

Joy handed off the coffee and baked goods to Emily and gave Heather one more hug. "I need to get back. I'll check with Emily later to see if there's any news. Don't stay here long. Kevin needs you way more than this store does."

Samantha's phone buzzed with a text. It was Amber, asking where she was. *Damn.* Samantha had forgotten that they had agreed to meet at the library on Saturday to work on a project. That had been Wednesday night, back when her world was normal and revolved around classes, friends, and having fun. Back when she thought she was being smart and responsible because she didn't drink and drive. Back before answering a text from Amber changed her life—and the lives of Kevin Wyland and the people who cared about him—forever.

Her response was swift and brief.

Sorry. Something came up. Can't make it.

It had been another sleepless night. She considered trying to call the hospital to see if they would tell her anything about Kevin's condition, but she was afraid they would ask who she was. She thought about calling an attorney to help her make sense of everything she was reading online, but she'd have to give a reason for her questions and she couldn't tell anyone, not even an attorney, what she'd done. And what was she going to do about her car? Was there a way to find someone who would repair it without asking how it had been damaged? So many questions, so many unknowns.

Maybe she could at least satisfy her curiosity about Kevin. She'd start with getting coffee at Joyful Cup. It was possible people who knew him would be in there talking about him and she could eavesdrop again.

She dressed quickly, scrunching her thick, curly blonde hair and applying makeup to the bruise on her cheek. It was still purple but getting lighter. She loaded her backpack as she had the day before—her laptop for a prop so she could sit in Joyful Cup for a while, her wallet, and keys—and headed out on foot. She wasn't ready to drive a car again.

This morning, she avoided looking down the street to the accident site as she crossed the busy road to get to Town Center. She didn't need to see the actual roadway. The vision of the impact was seared on her brain and likely would be forever.

As Samantha walked up to Joyful Cup, Joy was coming from the other direction. They reached the door at the same time, and Joy held it open for Samantha to enter.

"How's the project going?"

It took Samantha a moment to remember their conversation from yesterday, when she'd said she was having trouble getting started on a project. She was impressed with how Joy could remember those things, but Joy seemed to do it with everybody.

"I decided to work on something else for a while." It wasn't a total lie. She was working on trying to figure out how to get out of the biggest mess she'd ever been in.

"That's probably a good idea. And you know you're welcome to work in here as long as you like. Most of our weekend sports warriors have gone, so it's not quite as noisy as it was a while ago."

"I don't mind the noise." The noise was what she had been hoping for—noise in the form of conversation about Kevin. But there were still plenty of people in the shop, so she might still learn something.

Joy began clearing a recently-vacated table. "If you have time, you should go down to Wyland's. They've got some of the cutest puppies available for adoption. I know you probably can't manage another pet right now, but you could do some cuddling. I think puppy breath is great for creativity."

"I'll do that, thanks." Samantha managed a smile as she made her way to the counter to order an iced mocha.

She found a table in the middle of the room that would allow the best eavesdropping vantage point. Conversations swirled around her, but none was about the hit-and-run crash of two days ago or the condition of Kevin Wyland. Didn't any of these people know or care about him?

Kevin wanted to hear every detail of Heather's visit to the store. She did her best to oblige.

"There were plenty of people on the sidewalk checking out the pets. I'm not sure how many actual adoptions. People were coming into the store for other things. Emily, Jacob, and Nicole were busy, but there weren't any customers not being helped. Toby was happy to see me."

"Poor guy. He's got to be confused."

"Emily's taking good care of him. And at least he's in the store, instead of home by himself. He's getting plenty of attention. But he didn't understand why I didn't take him with me when I left."

"Did he try to follow you out?"

"Just for a few steps. I told him to go lie down and Nicole gave him some treats. He's milking it." Heather chuckled, thinking about how Toby was manipulating the store's employees into attention and snacks.

"That's my boy." Kevin returned to keeping the store adequately staffed. "Are all three of them going to work all day?"

"They'll all work while the animals are still there. I stopped at Joy's and picked up coffee and goodies for them, and I left those in the back room. I told Emily to close early tonight and to use her judgment about when to let Jacob and Nicole go home. I'll go by tomorrow and do the daily and weekly reports." The next day was Sunday and the store would be closed, so Heather could do the administrative work without any interruptions.

"Sales are going to be down."

"Maybe a little short-term. But our customers are loyal. Emily says people are asking about you."

"What's she telling them?"

"That your injuries were serious, you had surgery that went well, and in a few days we'll be updating our website and Facebook page with more details."

"We'll do that?" He sounded hopeful.

"*I'll* do that. Probably Monday."

"You could bring me the laptop—"

"No. You're not working. You need to rest. Besides, who knows what you'd end up posting while you're under the influence of pain medication?"

"Could be really good. I'd get us a lot of new followers."

Heather laughed at his impish expression. It didn't quite go with his bruised, swollen face, but that he managed it at all was a good sign. She kept her tone casual. "Joy told me that someone has set up a HelpNow account to raise money for us."

"We don't need charity." His rapid response was exactly what she expected.

"I think people just want to do something. I don't know much else about it. I'll try to find out next week."

There was a tap at the door and the orthopedic surgeon and his assistant came in. After an examination during which he dictated notes that sounded like gibberish to Heather, he announced that he was pleased with Kevin's progress.

Kevin was quick to reply. "So when can I get out of here?"

"We may be able to move you out of ICU and into a regular room by the middle of next week. We'll see how it goes. Of course, your neurologist will have to agree. And once the swelling has gone down in your face, we'll get you checked out by an ear, nose and throat specialist. I don't think you're going to need surgery on your nose, but we want to be sure."

"I'm going to be in here a week?"

"At least. Maybe two. You're doing well, but you're not out of the woods. I'll be back to check on you tomorrow." And he was gone.

Heather and Kevin sat in stunned silence. Two weeks in the hospital. How were they going to manage?

Under other circumstances, Samantha might have been entertained by some of the conversations she was overhearing. Today, she was just frustrated. She didn't care about sports or baby showers or remodeling projects. She wanted information about Kevin and she didn't know how to get it.

Finally a couple of sweaty cyclists came in and took the

table next to her. After several minutes of general conversation, one of them mentioned the accident. "He's lucky someone saw it and stopped. He could have been hit again."

"Yeah. Hit and run drivers are the scum of the earth. I hope they find the guy and give me just ten minutes alone with him."

"Get in line. He needs to suffer."

The words hit Samantha like one of the punches the two men wanted to throw. Because they had obviously been riding, she had been hoping they might know Kevin or at least know something about how he was. She wasn't expecting them to express such hatred for her. With trembling hands, she packed up her things and left her unfinished drink on the table. She knew the men had no idea who she was, but she couldn't sit and listen to them. She had to get outside.

Once on the sidewalk, she drew several deep breaths. The sound of barking dogs helped her regain her composure. What now? Why not follow Joy's advice and go to Wyland's? She would pretend to check out the puppies and get some cat food for Lucy. Surely she'd get an opportunity to ask about Kevin.

The scene at Wyland's was barely organized chaos. As the animal rescue group processed adoptions on the sidewalk in front of the store, people were inside buying food and various supplies and accessories for their new pets. Samantha petted several of the dogs and then entered the shop, which was clearly understaffed.

One of the clerks was apologizing to an older woman. "I'm sorry. We got the delivery yesterday, but it's all still in the back. If you don't mind waiting just a few minutes ..." Samantha watched as the clerk disappeared then reappeared with a case of canned food. Putting the case on the floor by the cash register, she used a box cutter to slash the plastic wrapping, pulled out four cans, and rang up the sale. The partial case stayed there as the clerk handled the following sale. For the next sale, she once again had to go to the back to get the product the customer wanted and went through the same process of opening a case. Another clerk was busy helping customers make selections inside the store and still another was outside offering advice to prospective adopters and helping to keep the sidewalk clean.

Samantha had been in the store enough to know that one or both of the owners were usually there, working alongside their employees, and now neither one was. And it was her fault.

She drew a deep breath. She wanted to turn around and leave. Instead, she walked toward the sales counter.

"Excuse me," she said to the next customer in line, "I'm not jumping ahead of you," then to the clerk, whose nametag identified her as Emily, "Can I help you get those cans of food out of your way and on the shelves?"

"I'm sorry?"

"I heard that Kevin is in the hospital. You're shorthanded and I have some free time. I'd like to help." Samantha was almost as surprised at her spur-of-the-moment offer as Emily appeared to be, but maybe working in the store would ease some of her guilt.

"Uh, sure. These go over there."

Samantha grabbed the two partial cases of pet food and got them out of Emily's way. "I'll figure it out."

Kevin was trying to absorb what the doctor had told them when Sergeant Grant appeared at the door.

"Good afternoon, Mr. Wyland. You're looking much better than you were the last time I saw you."

"They tell me I was a mess."

"Getting hit by a car has a way of doing that. How are you doing?" The sergeant's question included both of them but

Kevin answered.

"They did some repair work on my back yesterday. Doc said it went well, but I'm going to be here a while."

"And he's probably not going to win patient of the year," Heather added.

Sergeant Grant offered a sympathetic nod. "I understand. I wouldn't, either. Do you feel like answering a few questions?"

"Sure."

"Would you like to sit down?" Heather started to rearrange some of the things that were piled on the sofa to make a space for him.

"No, thanks, Mrs. Wyland, I'm fine. This won't take long." He pulled a small notebook out of his pocket and opened it. "Mr. Wyland—"

"Kevin."

"Kevin. Did you see the car that hit you?"

"No. Well, I don't think so. I don't remember being hit. I was riding my bike and the next thing I knew I was in a helicopter. I have these vague jumbled memories of flashing lights and sirens and people talking, but not of the car actually hitting me."

"Do you remember seeing any car driving erratically before you were hit?"

"No. It was early. There wasn't much traffic."

Sergeant Grant wrote briefly in his notebook, then flipped through the pages. "Let me tell you where we are in the investigation." He began to list the facts in a clipped, detached tone. "We have one witness who saw the crash, who saw you bounce over the car. He saw the car stop then drive away. We found some debris that we believe is from the car that hit you. We also found paint on your bicycle that likely came from the car. We're working on identifying the make and model of vehicle, but that will take a while. There were no cameras in the immediate vicinity, so we don't have any video of the crash. We have some video of about a half-mile on either side of the crash site. We're still analyzing that to see if we can ID the vehicle and maybe the driver. We're going to set up a Crimeline reward and put it out to the media, but we haven't released your name yet. Okay if we do that?"

"I guess. Sunshine, is there anyone else we need to call?"

"No. And word's getting around anyway."

The sergeant wrote a few words and then closed his notebook. "Thanks. Sometimes getting the victim's name out there can generate some tips."

"Do you think you'll find the guy?"

"We'll do our best. As I said, we don't have a lot to go on. But we're going to keep at it." He handed Heather a business card. "I think I gave you one of these already, but here's another one. If either of you can think of anything that might help, please call me."

Kevin watched until the sergeant was out of sight. His thoughts returned to the prognosis the surgeon had given them.

"I can't be in here two weeks. I don't even want to think about what this has already cost us." When they bought the high-deductible health insurance policy, it seemed like a good idea because they were both young and healthy. They hadn't thought about an accident like this.

"We don't have a choice, Kevin. You're going to be here as long as you need to be, as long as it takes for you to heal enough to go home."

"This is going to wipe out our savings and put us in debt for years. We could lose the store." His throat was so tight he could barely swallow.

"We won't lose the store. We'll handle it. We've been broke before. We got through then, we'll get through now."

"Always the optimist, aren't you, Sunshine?" He looked past her to the sofa, which was piled with things their friends had brought. "You've got quite a stash there."

"We're so blessed. Pastor Brett made sure I wasn't alone while you were in surgery. And everybody who came to sit with me brought something."

He clinched his fists and let the anger creep into his voice. "Blessed. Yeah."

7

Heather and Kevin were adjusting to the rhythm of the hospital—the frequent checks on Kevin by various nurses and technicians, the less-frequent visits by doctors, the janitors coming in to clean, the meal deliveries. Most of the noises that had at first seemed so foreign and sometimes alarming had faded into the background. Faces had become familiar. A small closet in the room was filling up with personal things—toiletries, snacks, books, and magazines.

Heather insisted on spending the night at the hospital and leaving for only a few brief hours during the day. After four nights, she was getting used to sleeping in yoga pants and a t-shirt on the sofa. One of the nurses made sure she had sheets, pillows, and blankets and showed her how to order extra meals from the hospital kitchen so she could eat with Kevin instead of going to the cafeteria. Heather had asked Pastor Brett to announce to the church that Kevin wasn't up to visitors and told Emily to say the same thing to anyone who might ask. It was just the two of them—and the medical team—in a cocoon that was oddly cozy amid the sterile medical equipment.

On Monday morning, they were watching the local news when the perfectly-groomed anchor said, "Winter Springs Police need your help solving a hit-and run crash. That story and more when we come back." Heather grabbed the remote and increased the volume, waiting impatiently for the commercials to end. Finally the anchor was back, first with a smile then adopting a serious expression as he began reading the next story.

"The Winter Springs Police Department is seeking the public's help in locating a hit-and-run driver who left a man in critical condition last week. The crash occurred about five a.m. last Thursday on State Road 434. The victim, Kevin Wyland of Winter Springs, remains in the hospital in serious condition but is expected to recover. If you have any information, call Crimeline at the number on your screen. You may remain anonymous and you may be eligible for a reward. In other news …"

Heather lowered the volume and tossed the remote down. "I hope this will do some good. It's so frustrating that no one saw the car."

"This guy needs to be caught. He can't get away with this."

"He won't get away with it. Even if the police don't find him, he'll be held accountable." Heather had total faith in God's judgment.

Kevin snorted. "I'd rather be around to see it."

"Of course. I would, too." Heather kept her tone even, hoping it would soothe the anger she heard in Kevin's voice. Maybe redirecting the conversation would help. "I'm just thankful that the man in the car behind you saw what happened in time to stop."

"Yeah."

They were silent for several minutes. From the expression on Kevin's face, Heather knew the subtle redirect hadn't worked. A complete subject change was in order.

"I talked with Emily while I was at the store yesterday." Heather had gone in on Sunday afternoon for a few hours to check the sales numbers, put together the bank deposit, and handle some other paperwork. "We figured out a temporary schedule that should work until you and I are out of here. She's going to open later and close earlier. Either Jacob or Nicole will be with her most of the time, so there will almost always be two people in the store whenever it's open. I put a sign up on the door before I left and I added a notice to the homepage of our website."

"I wish I could help you."

"Just concentrate on getting better. And call your mom." Kevin's mother lived in California with her second husband, a delightful man she had married last year after nearly 20 years as a widow. "I've told her there's nothing she can do here, but I'm not sure she believes me. She's checking flights."

"I'll call her. You've got enough on your hands without having to deal with her."

"I love your mom. It's just that I feel like I'd have to take care of her and—"

"I know. Taking care of me and the store is all you can handle. I understand. She will, too."

"One more thing. I think we should update our Facebook pages. That will be the easiest way for us to let everyone know how you're doing." Heather was more active on Facebook than Kevin was, and she knew he didn't like sharing personal information on social media. But several of their friends were already posting questions about Kevin's condition on her profile page. She needed to respond.

"I don't want the world to know that we're not home. If you put it out there that I'm in the hospital, people are going to know that you'll be with me and no one is in the house."

"We don't need to give a lot of details or even specifically say that you're still in the hospital—just that you're recovering, and we'll let people know when you're ready for visitors."

That seemed to appease his concern for security. "Okay. But no pictures."

"No pictures. At least not until you're gorgeous again."

Sound sleep still eluded Samantha. It felt like she'd been staring at the bedroom ceiling most of the night. Would it help to see where she had hit Kevin? It was worth a try, but she didn't want to drive there.

As the sky began to lighten, Samantha laced up her running shoes, tucked a house key and an identification card into the pocket of her athletic shorts, and headed out. She jogged at a comfortable pace, reaching the crash site in about 20 minutes. Wiping the sweat from her brow and pushing her damp hair off her neck, she stood on the sidewalk. Traffic whooshed by. A hawk screamed overhead. What had she expected to see?

There were a few pieces of trash on the grass under the large for sale sign that fronted the woods. Skid marks on the road—from her car? She didn't remember slamming on the brakes. She looked down the street, watching cars coming to-ward her as she had done that morning. Only these cars were staying in their lane, not swerving into the bike lane. Another scan of the grass. Was that a bike shoe? Could it be Kevin's? She resisted the temptation to pick it up.

One last look around. Everything seemed so ordinary. The sun was up, people were heading back to work on Monday morning. Hard to believe that such a life-changing event had occurred at this place just a few days ago. Why had she come here? She turned and began running home. She didn't realize how hard it was to run and cry at the same time.

A block away from her house, she slowed to a walk so she would cool down before going inside. Deep breaths helped her gain control of her emotions. She fed Lucy, showered, and was getting ready for school when her phone chimed. She had set up an alert so she would know if Kevin's name was mentioned on-line. Could he have died? Trembling, she picked up her phone. It took three tries before she was able to tap the link that popped up on her screen.

The Winter Springs Police Department was asking for help in finding the driver who hit Kevin and Crimeline was offering a reward for information. She stared at the news release that listed the date and time of the crash, along with how to make a report and claim the reward.

What information could anyone possibly have that the police didn't already know? Surely her car was the only thing that tied her to the crash and it was hidden in the garage. As long as she didn't say anything about it, no one would know what she'd done. But the car was a problem. Though it was technically drivable, it wasn't safe with the smashed windshield and she couldn't risk getting it repaired. She had to get rid of it. But how? She couldn't just abandon it—it would probably be found and traced back to her.

Maybe she could crash it. Hit a tree with the front right side to cover up the damage. But how fast would she have to be going to accomplish her purpose? Would investigators be able to tell the airbag was already deployed? And how badly would she be hurt?

The car had to be destroyed. Then she could say it had been stolen—but that would mean filing a false police report. How many crimes could she commit to avoid taking responsibility for the crash? She could make up another story about what happened to the car.

Could she burn it? The idea of setting a fire like that frightened her. What if it got out of control and started a brush fire? What if someone saw the burning car and the fire was put out before it could destroy the evidence of the crash? No, burning it was not an option.

But the opposite of fire would work. The solution was to dump the car in a lake—Florida has an abundance of lakes, many with large alligator populations that keep swimmers out of the water. If she could just get the car submerged, it was unlikely to be discovered.

How long had she been standing there, holding her phone, thinking? She focused on her phone to check the time. She had to hurry or she'd be late to school.

At least now she knew what she was going to do. When she got home from her classes this afternoon, she would figure out exactly how to accomplish it.

Kevin watched as Heather reviewed all the notes she had taken since his surgery. She set the notebook aside, picked up her laptop, and logged onto the internet.

"What are you doing?" His question was prompted as much by boredom as curiosity.

"I just want to find out a little more about some of the things the doctors said." Her fingers danced across the keyboard.

"Remember, Dr. Akerman told you not to do that."

"I know." She grinned and mimicked the doctor. "The internet is full of information that doesn't apply to Kevin. You'll read one article and think he's going to die tomorrow. You'll read another article and think he'll be back riding his bike in a week. The reality is that everyone's injuries are different and everyone heals differently."

"You were listening."

"Of course I was listening. And I was taking notes. But I never remember all my questions while he's here. And Dr. Akerman isn't your only doctor. Not all of them are as good at explaining things as he is."

"But they're probably all really good at billing." The cost of being in the hospital was never far from Kevin's mind. "When are you going to the store?"

"I thought I'd wait until this afternoon. I'll have lunch with you then run by the house and the store and get back before rush hour. What can I bring you?"

"Besides a ticket out of here? Stop by Joyful Cup and get us something for dessert tonight."

~

It was time. Samantha had to go to school and that meant opening the garage door to get Gram's car out. She knew the damage to her car wouldn't be visible to anyone who might be passing by on the street, but she was still nervous that one of the neighbors might stop for a chat, get close to the garage, and notice something.

She tossed her backpack into the passenger's seat and got behind the wheel of Gram's late model Honda. Ready with a polite smile and an excuse to avoid conversation if needed, she pressed the garage door button and waited anxiously, the gear shift already in reverse, while the door rolled up. As soon as she was clear of the garage door sensors, she pressed the button again. The door lowered, shielding her car from view. The next door neighbor looked up from the work he was doing in his front yard. She waved at him as she drove away.

Arriving at the massive University of Central Florida campus, Samantha found a parking space in a visitor's lot. Later she would deal with getting a parking decal for Gram's car. For now, she had to go to class. And pretend that everything was normal.

She removed her sunglasses—an extra pair she would use until she saw Amber and could get her favorite ones back—long enough to check her appearance in the rearview mirror. The bruise on her cheek had faded to light green and was barely noticeable under makeup. *Take a deep breath. You can do this.*

When she entered the classroom, Amber was already in her usual seat. Samantha took the seat next to her and busied herself with setting up her laptop.

Amber gave her an affectionate swat on the shoulder.

"Where were you this weekend?"

"Mostly home." That was true. Samantha kept her eyes on her computer as it booted up.

"Are you okay? What happened to you on Saturday? I got some research done, but I need your input."

"I'm fine. Long story. Sorry I stood you up." Samantha forced herself to glance at her friend. Instead of Amber, she saw Kevin flying off his bicycle and hitting her windshield. Her heart pounded. A dull roar filled her ears. What was happening to her?

Samantha blinked. The vision was replaced by Amber's face; the noise by Amber's voice.

"When do you want to do it?" Amber was obviously asking when Samantha wanted to reschedule their work session.

"Maybe Friday or Saturday?" Could Amber see the deep breaths she was taking? "Can I get back with you?" Before she made any commitments, she needed to be sure she had enough time to figure out how to dump her car and then do it.

"Sure. I'll send you what I've got so far." Amber typed on her computer, then reached down into her backpack. "Almost forgot. Here are your shades."

"Thanks." Samantha didn't want to touch the sunglasses. If she hadn't forgotten them, Amber wouldn't have texted her and she wouldn't be in the mess she was in. Her breathing quickened as she forced herself to take the glasses and put them in her own backpack. Apparently Amber noticed nothing amiss because she continued chatting.

"Hey, did you see that crash on Thursday morning? When I got the traffic alerts, I was worried about you."

"No. Didn't see it." The lie rolled easily off her tongue. "I got the traffic alerts, too. But I was already home."

~

"You know what I just remembered?" Heather had helped get Kevin's lunch arranged on his tray and her own on the table beside the sofa when a thought struck her. "Yesterday was Palm Sunday. This is Holy Week."

"You're right. I forgot, too." Kevin picked up his napkin. "I told Brett I'd help with setting up for the Maundy Thursday service."

"I think he knows you're not going to be able to. But I was supposed to help with the Easter egg hunt. We're stuffing plastic eggs on Wednesday."

"You can still do that."

"You keep trying to get rid of me, Kevin. What's going on here that you don't want me to know about?" She took a bite of her sandwich, smiling as she chewed and waited for him to answer.

Kevin stabbed at the grilled chicken breast. "Come on. You know everything that's going on here. But you can't just hang around here. You've got other things to do, other commitments."

"You're my commitment. I don't mind leaving you for a short time to go home and shower and check on the store, but I'm not leaving you for hours to sort toys and candy. And I'm sorry that we're going to miss the Holy Week services, but that's just the way it is. So stop trying to get me to leave." Frustration and the edge of tears colored her voice.

"Okay." He held his hands up in a gesture of surrender. "I just—"

"I know. But if I was the one in that hospital bed, where would you be?"

"Right where you are."

"Exactly. I love it when you make my point for me. Now, let's have our lunch." Her emotions were back under control.

Shortly after they finished eating, a nurse came in to help

Kevin take his doctor-ordered walk to the end of the hall and back. She easily deflected his resistance to using the walker and made cheerful small talk as she guided him out of the room. It was an exhausting, painful part of the recovery process, but his spirits seemed high as he made jokes about his slow pace.

Once he was back in bed, he closed his eyes. "I could ride 20 miles without feeling this tired."

Heather stroked his face. "Get some rest. It will get easier."

This would be a good time for her to leave, but she settled on the sofa. Just for a few minutes, she told herself. She would watch him doze for a few minutes, then she would leave and be back before he woke up.

Heather didn't remember closing her eyes, but when she woke up Kevin was watching her, an expression of concern on his still bruised face. She sat up and tried to orient herself.

"I must have fallen asleep."

"You did. So did I."

"I'm sorry. What time is it? I should get to the store."

"I think you needed the rest. Are you feeling okay?"

"Yes, why?" She started to get to her feet, but felt light-headed, so she sat back down.

"You look a little off. A little pale."

"I'm just tired." After a few deep breaths, her head was clearing. "I'm all right."

"Why don't you skip going to the store? Stay with me."

She didn't want to admit that she didn't feel up to fighting traffic and dealing with whatever business was waiting for her, but he probably sensed it. Still, she couldn't give in too easily. "First you want to get rid of me, now you don't want me to leave."

"Hey, I'm an injured man. I'm entitled to change my mind."

"Well, if you insist, I'll stay." She leaned back, wondering why her nap had left her feeling drained rather than refreshed.

Don't let me be sick. I can't get sick right now.
Sleep overtook her again.

It had been a totally unremarkable, ordinary day.

On her first day back at school since the accident, Samantha's classes went as planned. No one noticed—or, at least, mentioned—the traces of the fading bruise on her cheek. No one asked why she wasn't parked in her usual lot or driving her own car. No one said anything about her being quieter than she typically was. And, unlike the people in the stores at Town Center, no one was talking about Kevin Wyland having been hit by a car. Only Amber said something about the crash, and that was simply to confirm Samantha's safety.

When she got home that afternoon, Samantha decided to leave Gram's car outside rather than open the garage. Parking in the driveway was frowned on by the homeowners association, but she could probably get away with it for a few days—just until she made her own car disappear.

Entering the house through the front door, she dropped her backpack and grabbed the mailbox key. She hadn't picked up the mail since before the crash and the box was probably full with the catalogs Gram loved—and it was. As she walked back from the central mailbox, the next door neighbor was outside again. She smiled and waved at him, hoping to get past him without any significant engagement. No such luck.

"Driving your grandma's car, I see."

Samantha answered without stopping. "Yes. I don't think it's good for it to let it sit too long without being driven."

"Are you going to keep it?"

"I don't know. That's up to my mom." She knew she was being rude by continuing to walk, but she didn't want to get into an extended conversation.

"You know you'll likely get a letter for parking in the driveway."

Samantha stopped. Yes, the homeowners association sent letters to residents who violated any of the rules of the meticulously maintained community, but why had he brought that up? Gram had described the couple who lived next door as good neighbors—friendly, helpful, but never meddling. Except now it felt like he was being intrusive.

"I'll get it back in the garage. The door remote wouldn't work when I got home." It was the only excuse she could think of.

"Want me to check it for you?"

"No!" The refusal came out harsher than she intended. She softened her tone and tried again. "No, thank you. I'll figure it out."

"Well, if you need any help—"

"I know where you are." Forcing a smile, she finished the sentence for him and resumed walking toward her front door. "Thanks. See you later." She hoped he wasn't offended, but it wouldn't take him more than a minute to determine that nothing was wrong with the garage door opener. There was no way she was going to let him see inside the garage and, in the process, see her damaged BMW. She couldn't let that happen.

Once inside the house, she tried to put everything related to the crash out of her mind. She had several reading assignments she needed to complete this week so she loaded them up on her laptop. But the words on the screen weren't making any sense. Instead of reading, she found herself searching Google Maps for a boat ramp in an isolated area.

She identified three locations that might work for ditching her car. She'd use Gram's car to check them out tomorrow in the daylight and choose one that she would return to in the dark in her car. Feeling as though she'd accomplished something, she closed her laptop and decided to walk over to Town Center. Maybe she could help out at Wyland's again and get some news about Kevin.

Even though it was after six o'clock, thanks to daylight saving time, the sun was still high above the horizon as she approached the pet supply store. When she reached for the door, it wouldn't open. That's when she noticed the sign taped to the glass:

> *Temporary Hours*
> *10:30 a.m. – 6 p.m. – Monday through Friday*
> *9 a.m. – 6 p.m. – Saturday*
> *Closed Sunday*
> *We apologize for any inconvenience.*

The sign with the store's regular hours was still on the window. With Kevin in the hospital, they would be short on staff. Samantha knew enough about business to know what it meant to a small retailer to lose three or four hours of sales time per day. In addition to what she had done to him physically, her carelessness was costing Kevin a lot of money.

Nobody swam in Lake Jesup. Though the large lake was relatively shallow, the alligator population was so dense that it wasn't safe for swimmers. But as part of the St. Johns River, it was popular with boaters and had plenty of public boat ramps. The areas around those ramps had been dredged out to provide more depth for launching boats.

After finding Wyland's Pet Food and Supplies closed, Samantha walked home and went through the motions of normal life—feeding Lucy, preparing her own meal, cleaning up. Then she sat down at her computer to study an aerial map of Lake Jesup. She identified two boat ramps that might work for disposing of her car.

She would have to dump her car at night to reduce the risk of being seen, but she wanted to check out the boat ramps during the day to figure out which one would be better. With only one class the next day, she had plenty of time to finish her plan in the afternoon and then execute it after dark.

Maybe then she would be able to sleep.

~

"I know you don't want visitors, so I'm not going to stay. I just wanted to bring you this." Joy carried a Joyful Cup box of baked goods into Kevin's hospital room. "I'm told it's a good idea to bribe the nurses with goodies."

Heather sprang up from the sofa, reaching out to embrace Joy as she took the box. "You are so sweet. You didn't have to do this."

"Pick out what you want and take the rest to the nurses' station. Leave the box where people can see it—it's good advertising." Joy returned Heather's hug and looked past her to smile at Kevin. "How are you feeling?"

"Not as bad as I was. And I'm walking. I have to use the walker, but I'm mobile."

"They're not letting him be lazy," Heather added. "We go for several walks a day. And we found out this morning that his nose should heal without surgery. The neurologist is monitoring his head injury and still thinks that's going to heal on its own. We're expecting to be out of ICU in another day or two."

"I love hearing good news." Joy smiled at her friends as she smoothly announced her departure. "Well, like I said, I'm not staying. When you're ready for company, let me know. And if there's anything I can do ..." Even as she made the offer, Joy knew that the most important thing she could do was to be a friend who would listen and offer guidance to both of them in the coming days and weeks.

Samantha stood at the edge of the lake. It was a beautiful day, warm, with a gentle breeze—a perfect day to be outside. Gram would have called it chamber of commerce weather. Looking out across the calm water, she saw two men fishing in a skiff and further out an airboat skimmed over the lake's surface. Near the shore, an alligator glided slowly. Though only its head was visible, from its wake she guessed the creature was probably nine or ten feet long. It didn't seem interested in leaving the water, but she still took several steps back.

This boat ramp would work. She had to drive through a

residential area to get to it, but there were no homes or other buildings within a quarter mile. Even though it was a public facility, it likely wasn't as heavily used as the other one she'd been to. The ramp itself was a concrete road that sloped gently into the water, wide enough for at least two vehicles and bordered on both sides by sandy Florida scrub.

She took one last look around. It would be very dark when she came back and she needed to remember the landscape.

I can do this. I have to.

She headed back to the gravel parking lot at the top of the ramp. As she got into Gram's car, a pickup truck hauling a boat pulled in. The driver waved. She smiled and nodded, trying to be inconspicuous as she drove away.

Kevin was bored. Heather was on the sofa, tapping away on her laptop, responding to social media posts and emails from people who wanted to know how he was doing. He was just lying in his hospital bed, waiting for time to pass. He didn't want to watch TV—there were only a few shows he liked and, besides, as soon as he got interested in a program, someone would interrupt to take his vitals, bring him food or medication, or get him up for one of the exhausting walks he had to take. Heather had brought in a small speaker and plugged her phone into it, so music played softly in the background, but listening to that wasn't enough to occupy him.

"Have you heard anything from Sergeant Grant?" He knew he was distracting her but he couldn't help himself.

"No, not since he was here on Saturday." Heather closed her computer. "I hope he's getting lots of leads from Crimeline and is busy chasing them all down."

"I really want the piece of garbage who did this to me—to us—to be caught. I want him prosecuted." How many times had he said that in the past few days? Probably too many.

"So do I. But remember what Sergeant Grant said about how hard it is to catch hit-and-run drivers. Even if they arrest him, it could take a while for them to prosecute him."

"I know. I'm just frustrated, stuck in here. The bills are racking up, sales are down in the store."

Heather leaned forward. "Sales are *not* down in the store. We had a normal weekend. They might be a little off this week because we're closing early, but we'll make it up."

"It's going to take us years to pay off the hospital bill." Even with the amazing generosity of people who had donated to the HelpNow account.

"Maybe. But that's okay, because you're going to be okay. Let's just take things one day at a time and trust God."

Trust God? Would that be the same God that allowed me to be hit by a car?

Kevin couldn't bring himself say those words out loud—it would hurt Heather and he didn't want to do that. His faith had never been as deep as hers and now he was wondering if the whole church and religion thing was all a sham.

Samantha stood in the garage, staring at her car. Where should she start?

Though the car was drivable as it was, it would be easier to handle without the airbag fabric flowing out of the steering wheel. Back to the kitchen for a pair of heavy-duty scissors and a large black trash bag. She trimmed away the airbag and stuffed it into the trash bag.

Next she removed all her personal belongings from the trunk, the back seat, the console and glovebox, loading everything in a cardboard box. With her mind on autopilot, she scooped up an umbrella, workout clothes, books, and other odds and ends. She stashed the box in a corner of the garage to sort it out later. Then she scraped her school parking decal from the window and put it in an envelope. She would need that to get a student permit for Gram's car.

With the car ready to go, she gathered supplies: a screwdriver to remove the license plate after she got to the boat ramp, a flashlight, one of the rocks Gram used as a landscape decoration to put on the gas pedal, a water bottle so she'd have something to drink on the long walk home. Then she chose her clothes—black yoga pants and a navy long-sleeved t-shirt. Searching through Gram's closet, she found a black scarf that would work to cover her blonde hair.

She took her spare car key—one that had no identification or other keys attached—from the key rack next to the garage door. She would use that when she drove to the boat ramp. Using the kitchen stepstool, she loosened the light bulb in the garage so it would remain dark when she opened the door, reducing the chances of someone seeing her drive away.

Finally there was nothing left to do except wait. She calculated that the best time to dump the car would be between one and two o'clock in the morning because no one was likely to be using the boat ramp and people in the houses across the lake would be asleep. Though traffic would be light, it was possible a police officer might see her as she was driving to the boat ramp and question her about the damaged windshield. It was a chance she'd have to take.

The minutes ticked by at an excruciatingly slow pace. She considered leaving early to get it done. No, it was better to stick with her original plan. If only the knots in her stomach would ease. Unable to sit still, she roamed around the house. She looked at the framed pictures Gram had on almost every surface, picked up and put down the knickknacks that Gram treasured. She tried to focus on something—anything—that would distract her from how slowly time was passing.

Then it was one o'clock. Her heart began to pound. Time to go.

Trying to still her trembling hands, she drove carefully, using side streets as much as possible. As she expected on a weeknight, few other vehicles were on the road at that hour. Still, she held her breath each time she saw another car until she was sure it wasn't a cop.

Her heart was racing when she arrived at the boat ramp. A single street light illuminated the empty parking area. She drove to a corner of the lot where she could park in a shadow, the gravel crunching loudly under her tires. Pulling the flashlight and screwdriver out of her backpack, she began removing the license plate from the rear of the car. She should have loosened the screws at home; they were tighter than she realized. In spite of the mild night and temperature in the low 60s, her entire body was perspiring, probably from a combination of stress and exertion. Did she really need to remove the license plate? Probably not, because the car could still be identified without it. But not having a plate could slow down the ID process and provide her with some additional deniability if the car was ever found.

Finally the plate came loose. She wiped her face with her sleeve and got back in the car, putting the screwdriver and license plate in her backpack, holding out the flashlight.

Was she really doing this? Yes. She had no choice.

She drove about halfway down the boat ramp, to the point just before where the pavement began sloping, stopping in the center of the wide strip of concrete. She lowered all the windows so the car would fill with water and sink quickly. With the engine running, she put the gear shift in neutral, turned the headlights off, grabbed her backpack, and got out of the car. She dropped her backpack on the ground then turned back to the car to place the rock from Gram's yard on the gas pedal. As the engine revved, she slammed the door, reached through the window, pulled the gear shift into drive and leapt back as the car jumped forward.

The car raced down the ramp. The splash wasn't as loud as she thought it would be. She watched as the car seemed to float for a few seconds, then disappeared. Picking up her backpack, she walked slowly toward the ramp's edge. Light from the half moon reflected on the rippling water. Were those alligator eyes staring at her with curiosity—or condemnation? She didn't want to find out. She turned and walked briskly up the ramp to the road. The hardest part was done. Now she just had to get home.

The road through the residential area surrounding the boat ramp had few streetlights, no sidewalks, and lots of trees blocking the moonlight, making it a challenging trek. She carried the flashlight but was reluctant to turn it on, choosing instead to walk slowly. She was grateful that there was no traffic, no one to wonder why she was walking alone in the middle of the night. After she'd gone about a half-mile, she pulled Gram's scarf off of her head, figuring that would make her look less suspicious.

It was another mile before she reached a main road with streetlights, sidewalks, and businesses. Most were closed but the exteriors were lit. Though she could now see where she was walking and could quicken her pace, she felt less safe on this road than she had on the dark side road. She was still about eight or ten miles from home.

In all her planning, she hadn't given much thought to how far the walk home was. She pulled her phone out to check the time—almost three o'clock. At this rate, it would be at least five before she got home. She had intended to walk home so there would be no record of her being out, but could she walk that distance in the middle of the night without attracting the attention of either a criminal or the police? Maybe, but what if she got attacked? What if a cop stopped and asked her what she was doing? Once that train of thought began, it took only a few seconds to decide to call for a ride.

The lights of a 24-hour convenience store shown a few blocks in the distance. It would be a secure place to wait for a SafeRide driver to pick her up.

The clerk in the store showed no curiosity when she asked if it was okay for her to wait inside for her ride. His response of a wordless shrug was fine. She didn't want to talk, she didn't want to be remembered. When she saw her driver pull up, she quickly left the store without saying anything else.

The driver was an older man, possibly in his 70s, and considerably more talkative than the taciturn store clerk. He confirmed her name and destination, pulled out of the store's parking lot, and began chatting.

"Beautiful night, isn't it? The weather is always so nice this time of year."

"Yes." Samantha stared out the window, hoping her short answer would be the end of the conversation. It wasn't.

"Did your car break down?"

"Yes." The lie was quick and easy. It was a good reason for needing a ride at this hour.

"I thought so. Most of my riders have been drinking and I pick them up at a bar. But when I saw you, I figured you'd had car trouble."

"Hmm." Should she praise his intuition? No, the less she said, the better.

He prattled on, telling her stories of other riders, praising the invention of ride sharing services. He didn't seem to notice—or care—that she was barely listening. Under other circumstances, she might have been sympathetic to the fact that he was probably lonely, but tonight she just wanted to get home.

The car was barely stopped in front of her house before she had the door open. She tapped the payment app on her phone, hopped out, smiled briefly as he told her to take care, and got inside as quickly as she could.

Without turning on any lights, she headed to her bedroom and tossed her backpack in the corner. She kicked off her shoes, crawled under the covers still dressed, and fell into an exhausted sleep.

As she often did during the morning rush, Joy was clearing and wiping tables, chatting with customers, and letting her staff handle the counter. Her hands-on style was a key reason Joyful Cup had such a loyal following. She knew her customers, knew their habits and preferences, knew what was going on in their lives. So she was surprised to see Heather come in shortly after eight o'clock. But before Joy had a chance to ask why Heather was there so early instead of being at the hospital with Kevin, Heather put a hand to her mouth and rushed to the restroom.

Joy casually moved across the dining area so she would be near the door when Heather came out. She heard the toilet flush, water run, and the automatic paper towel dispenser whirr. The door opened slowly.

"Heather, are you okay?" Joy kept her voice low.

"I don't know what happened." Heather wiped her pale forehead with a damp paper towel. "I was fine and then all of a sudden I was sick."

"You've been under a lot of stress. It does strange things to us."

"I guess." Heather took a breath. "I wanted a cup of coffee before I went to the store, but ..."

"Come, sit down. Let me get you a cup of tea. I've got a chamomile white tea that should help settle your stomach." Joy guided Heather to one of the overstuffed loveseats toward the back. "Relax. I'll be back in a few minutes."

Heather was leaning back, staring at the ceiling when Joy placed a black and white filigreed mug with Philippians 4:13 in bold letters on the side table. "Careful, it's hot."

Color returned to Heather's face as she sipped the mild brew. "This is good, thanks. I'm feeling better. I'm just tired. Sleeping on the sofa at the hospital is exhausting."

Joy sat next to Heather. "I can imagine. How's Kevin?"

"Improving. He should be moved to a regular room today. That's why I'm here so early. I went home for a shower, and I wanted to do a few things in the store and then get back to the hospital before the doctor comes in."

"That's great news. Is he up to visitors?"

"I think so. He didn't want any at first, but he's feeling better and I think he's bored. He worries about the store, about me, about how long it's taking the police to find the driver who hit him. Our pastor has been in a few times, and I think Kevin appreciated that." Heather cradled the mug in both hands. "We both just want to get him home."

"Of course you do. But it's only been a week."

"Is that all? It seems like longer."

"How's the investigation going?" Joy probably knew as much as Heather did since Sergeant Grant had been coming in almost every day, but she wanted to keep Heather talking so she would sit still for a while.

"I'm not sure. Crimeline is offering a reward for information, but we haven't heard from Sergeant Grant in a few days. He told us these investigations can take a long time and that hit-and-runs often never get solved. Kevin didn't handle that well." Heather smiled wryly as Joy chuckled.

"Kevin's not the most patient guy, is he? Sergeant Grant's a good cop. He'll keep working on this."

"He seems to be. I like him." Heather drained her cup. "Thanks for this, Joy. I'm feeling better. I need to get over to the store."

"Take care of yourself." Joy hesitated, then added, "You know, there might be another reason, other than exhaustion, for you being sick."

"I hope not. I don't know if they'd let me be in the hospital with Kevin if I have a bug."

"What I'm thinking about isn't contagious."

"What?" Heather's expression was blank, then comprehension dawned. "Oh, no. No. That can't be."

"Whatever you say." With a knowing smile, Joy picked up the cup. "Just take it easy. Let me know if they get Kevin moved today. I'll stop in to see him tomorrow."

It was almost noon when Samantha woke from a fitful sleep, still in the clothes she'd worn the night before. She'd missed class again, but the nightmares weren't quite as bad as they had been. For the first time in a week, she was feeling almost safe. There were just a few more things she needed to do to complete her plan.

Retrieving her backpack from the corner of her room, she pulled out the license tag she'd removed before dumping her car in the lake. Could she damage it beyond legibility?

Ducking around her bicycle in the garage, she took a hammer out of Gram's toolbox and knelt on the floor in the space her car had occupied. After just three strikes on the license plate, she stopped. Could the noise that echoed through the garage be heard outside? All she was doing was denting the numbers— what was the point in that? She got to her feet, put the hammer away, and added the tag to the trash bag that held the airbag she'd cut from the steering wheel last night. With brisk motions, she tied the bag closed and dropped it into the garbage can. The trash would be picked up tomorrow and by Saturday the bag should be in a landfill, mixed in with thousands of pounds of garbage.

Without the evidence of her damaged car and any witnesses, no one could prove that she had hit Kevin Wyland. The only thing left to do was to decide on a story for why she didn't have her BMW anymore.

The diesel engine roared and the equipment banged as the garbage truck made its way down the street, picking up cans and dumping their contents into the hopper, pausing every so often to compact the garbage. Samantha watched through the living room window as the robotic arm emptied her can and set it back down in the driveway. Then the truck rounded the corner and was out of sight, taking away the last evidence of what she'd done.

Relief. Why didn't she feel more relief?

She wondered how Kevin was doing. Neither the store's website nor its Facebook page contained any new information, just what had been posted earlier in the week about the store's temporary hours and to contact the police or Crimeline with any information about the crash. A check of Kevin and Heather's personal Facebook profiles revealed nothing. If they were talking about the accident, they were doing it privately.

It was Friday and Samantha didn't have any classes. If she went to Wyland's to buy cat food, maybe she could find out more.

~

When he heard the nurse enter the room, Kevin quickly raised his finger to his lips. "Shhhh," he whispered. "She's sleeping."

He glanced at Heather who was curled up in a recliner with her eyes closed.

"No, I'm not." Heather stretched, pushed the blanket off, and reached for the button to bring the recliner upright. To the nurse, she said, "Do what you need to do. Don't worry about me." Then to Kevin, "I'm glad you're out of ICU, but I liked the sofa there better than this chair."

Yesterday's move out of ICU had been a challenge. The personal items Heather had been accumulating were more than she could carry and the hospital didn't have any type of cart for her to use to transport them. Kevin insisted she pile things on his bed, in spite of the disapproving look from the nurse. When they got to the regular room, they were both surprised at how small and sparsely furnished it was—just his bed, the standard overbed table, and a single reclining chair without even a side table. Along one wall was a narrow built-in cabinet with a counter. Heather was able to display some of the cards he'd received on the counter and just barely got her personal items stored in the cabinet.

"I'm sorry, Sunshine. I keep telling you to go home."

"And I keep telling you I'm staying. I'll go home when you can come with me."

"I never realized you could be so stubborn."

The nurse—a new one they hadn't met before—updated the status board and moved to the bed to take Kevin's vitals. "For what it's worth, her kind of stubbornness is good for you, Mr. Wyland. Patients always do better when they have support. And we're going to do our best to get you out of here as soon as possible, so you can both go home. How are you feeling?"

"Fine. Still sore, but it's getting better."

"Good. I'll be back after breakfast and we'll get you up for a walk."

"I'm looking forward to it." He watched her leave, then

turned to Heather. "You can't have gotten much sleep."

"I got enough." She stood up and stretched again. "I could use a massage."

"Just as soon as I'm able ..." He leered at her as he let the words trail off.

Heather picked up her phone and made a show of ignoring him as she checked her email. "It's Good Friday. Looks like we're going to be celebrating Easter here."

"You should go to church." He knew how much Heather loved Easter. She often said it was the proof of her faith. She loved going to sunrise services and then hosting a casual Easter lunch for friends who didn't have family nearby. It had become a tradition for them.

"Maybe I will. We'll see. You might get some visitors. I've told everyone that we won't be having our annual Easter dinner this year, but I think some of them would like to come by if you're up to it."

"I think I'm ready for them." Most of the swelling from his broken nose had subsided and the bruises were fading. His fractured pelvis and broken ribs were still painful when he moved, but it wouldn't hurt to lie in bed and have a conversation with some friends. And it might help distract him from his angry thoughts about the driver that hit him.

There was a tap on the door followed by a cheerful "Good morning!" from one of the hospital's foodservice workers. As he placed the tray on Kevin's bedside table, Heather dropped her phone on the chair, mumbled "Excuse me," and rushed into the bathroom.

Samantha towel-dried her hair and studied her face in the mirror. She looked better than she had in days, probably because she'd gotten more rest the night before than she had since the accident. The nightmares hadn't ended, but there were fewer of them. The bruise on her cheek was no longer visible and the shadows under her eyes were barely noticeable. She could do without makeup today and in the mid-afternoon warmth her hair would be dry by the time she walked to Town Center.

The shopping center was busier than usual, bustling with people either preparing for Easter or just enjoying the first day of a three-day weekend. Samantha stopped in Joyful Cup for a small coffee, hoping to have a chance to ask Joy about Kevin, but Joy wasn't there. She saw a few other familiar faces, but no one she felt comfortable talking to. Back to her initial plan— she'd go buy cat food.

As she approached Wyland's, the door opened and her next door neighbor stepped out. "Well, hello, Samantha. Are you coming to get Lucy some of her gourmet food?"

"It's the only kind she'll eat."

"Your grandmother spoiled that cat."

"My grandmother spoiled everyone." Samantha was surprised at how easily the banter came. Maybe it was because it was easy to speak fondly of Gram.

"Indeed she did. We miss her. Say, did you get the garage door opener fixed?"

"The what—oh, yes." For a second, she forgot the excuse she'd given him for leaving Gram's car in the driveway. "I don't know what was wrong with it. The next time I tried it, it worked." It wasn't a total lie. Best to change the subject. She gestured to the bag he was carrying. "I didn't know you had a pet."

"We don't. Our daughter just got her kids a puppy, so my wife sent me over here to get some toys and treats for it." He looked in the bag and shook his head. "I probably bought more than I should have, but I figured they could use the extra business, what with the owner in the hospital."

"That's very thoughtful of you. Do you know how he's

doing?" Samantha seized the opportunity to learn more.

"Okay, I guess. It's a shame that happened. I hope they find the criminal that hit him."

"I hope so, too." What else could she say? *I hope they don't find "the criminal" because I don't want to go to jail.* To put an end to the conversation, she moved toward the door. "Well, you have a nice day. Enjoy the puppy."

As he waved and walked away, Samantha pulled the door open. Emily looked up from a display of pet dishes she was arranging into simple, utilitarian stacks, smiling warmly. "Hello! It's nice to see you again."

"You remember me?"

"Of course I remember you. It was so crazy in here on Saturday. You're the angel that appeared and began stocking shelves. I can't thank you enough. It's Samantha, right?"

"Yes. I was glad to help. I worked in retail stores when I was in high school. It was fun." Samantha looked around. The only other person in the store was a customer browsing by the racks of collars and pet costumes. A large black dog lumbered out from behind the counter. Samantha held out her hand for him to sniff and asked, "Is there anything else I can do?"

Emily looked puzzled. "We're not hiring right now. Toby, go lie down."

"Oh, I'm not looking for a job. I just—you know, I heard about the accident. My grandmother used to come in here. She died a few months ago. She really liked the owners. So I thought I would help if I could." Samantha wasn't sure if she was making any sense.

"I'm sorry about your grandmother."

"Thanks. She was a wonderful lady." Samantha pointed to the pet dishes Emily had been positioning on a display case. "No offense, but would you like me to arrange those? They're really cute, but people can't see them stacked like that."

Emily raised her hands in mock surrender. "Have at it. Setting up displays isn't what I do best. Heather usually does that, but she's spending most of her time at the hospital with Kevin."

It was the opening that Samantha was looking for. "How's he doing?"

"He's getting better. They moved him out of ICU yesterday. Heather's still not sure when they're going to let him go home."

"Is he going to be okay?" She was already working on the display, trying to sound nonchalant.

"Heather says the doctors are optimistic, but it's going to be a while. He had some pretty serious injuries." She looked toward the door as another customer came in. "Excuse me."

"Sure. Go ahead. I'll do this." Samantha continued moving the dishes around, creating a variety of heights and angles designed to showcase the products. She finished that and decided to tackle the adjacent display of Easter baskets for pets while Emily helped the customers.

Samantha was straightening up the racks of pet-related books as Emily was checking out the only customer left in the store. If the store stayed empty for a while, maybe she'd have a chance to find out more about Kevin. She groaned to herself when she heard the door open again, then froze when Emily spoke.

"Heather! I didn't know you were coming in this afternoon."

"Joy's at the hospital with Kevin so I thought I'd come get some work done."

Samantha knew she should turn and greet Heather, but she couldn't move.

"I'm glad you're here. I want you to meet someone. This is Samantha, the angel I told you about who came in last Saturday and started stocking shelves. And now she's back, doing the displays. Samantha, this is Heather, Kevin's wife."

Somehow Samantha managed to turn away from the racks. She wondered if her smile looked as wooden as it felt. She should say something, but what?

"The displays look wonderful. You're so kind to do this." Heather extended her hand.

Samantha didn't want to take Heather's hand, but she knew she had to. She searched for something to say. "If my grandmother were still alive, she'd be in here, too."

"That's right. You're Linda Kenyon's granddaughter, aren't you? I'm sorry I didn't place you at first." Heather released Samantha's hand. "Kevin loved to tease your grandmother."

"I know. And she loved it. She always spoke highly of both of you. She would've been upset about what happened to him. I hope he's doing okay."

"He's improving every day."

Samantha wasn't comfortable asking Heather for more information and she didn't know what else to say. "That's good. Well … I, uh, I need to go."

"Thank you again. You have no idea how much this means to us."

Samantha smiled weakly and headed to the door. "I'm glad I could help."

Once outside, she took several deep breaths of the fresh spring air, then began walking home. She was halfway there before she realized she had forgotten to buy cat food.

"I'd offer you a seat but there isn't one. Go ahead and sit on the bed." Kevin had been for a walk and was now sitting in the room's only chair, the recliner Heather had slept in, with a blanket over his lap.

"I don't mind standing. Besides, I understand one of the

major rules of hospital visits is to never sit on the bed." Joy put her purse on the narrow counter and leaned against the wall.

"How did you manage to get away from your shop on a Friday afternoon?"

"I have a good team. Just like you do. How are you doing?"

"I'm making progress. I should get out of here next week. And I know I have a good team, but they can only carry the load so far." Kevin adjusted his chair slightly.

"They're stronger than you think. You need to focus on healing. Your store will be fine."

"You sound like Heather."

"And we're both right. Accept it."

"I can accept that, but I'm having a hard time accepting all of this. You know?" He waved his arm in a broad gesture. "I was minding my own business, not doing anything wrong. And some jackass nearly kills me and turns our lives upside down."

"It doesn't make any sense, does it?"

"That's one way to put it. It might make more sense if they could find the guy. He should be in jail." Kevin tried to tamp down the anger he knew was coming through his voice.

"The police are doing everything they can. Sergeant Grant was in my shop the other day. He said they haven't gotten any tips from Crimeline. They're still waiting for lab reports on the debris they found at the scene. It takes time, but they're working on it."

"Yeah. Time." Kevin didn't want to hear it. He changed the subject. "I'm worried about Heather. She's not getting enough rest, sleeping here in the hospital. This morning, it sounded like she was vomiting in the bathroom. She said she wasn't, but I'm afraid she's getting sick and doesn't want me to know it."

There was something tender and knowing in Joy's smile. "I saw her yesterday and she seemed fine. You're right, she's tired. But I don't think she'd sleep any better if she were at home by herself. You two are such an in sync couple. You get your strength from each other. She needs to be here with you and I think you need her here."

"You're right." It was a sheepish admission. "I keep telling her to go home and I'm glad when she doesn't. But I'm still worried."

"Don't be. Worry doesn't help. It's almost like praying for the wrong thing to happen."

"I never thought of it that way." After a beat, he added, "I haven't been doing much praying."

"That's okay. Plenty of people are praying for you. But you might want to try it."

"I'm not sure God wants to hear what I have to say."

Joy pushed herself off the wall and took a step toward Kevin. "God always wants to hear what we have to say. But maybe, instead of you talking to God, you should spend some time listening to him. It's amazing what we hear when we listen."

"Thanks for the advice, Joy. And thanks for coming by." He looked out the door to avoid meeting her eyes. Her words had struck a nerve, but he didn't want to discuss it. "I don't mean to be rude, but I'm tired. I think I'll take a nap."

After Joy left, Kevin fumbled with the button on the chair and managed to get himself into a semi-reclining position. Though he closed his eyes, he wasn't sleeping. Or praying. He was visualizing vengeance on the driver that did this to him.

Heather knew she wasn't functioning at full capacity. She and Emily were in the store's small office, going over the week's per-formance report. Emily was talking but Heather only heard part of the positive news. When Emily paused, Heather knew she had to say something.

"The sales numbers look great, in spite of the short hours."

Heather forced energy she didn't feel into her voice.

Emily nodded. "Our regular customers are making a point to get in while we're open. I think a lot of them are buying more than they usually do. The pet Easter baskets are selling well—that was a great idea. And everyone is asking about Kevin."

"That's—" Heather paused. She felt tears welling up and she didn't want to cry. After a few deep breaths, she was back in control. "I don't know what to say. I don't know how we'll ever be able to thank everyone. Especially you."

"I'm just doing my job."

"You're doing so much more and you know it." Heather picked up a stack of mail and stuffed it into her purse. "I'll go through this later. I need to get back to the hospital."

But first she had to make a stop. At a drug store. To buy a pregnancy test.

eather set the alarm on her phone for five-thirty. She wanted to be awake and out of the hospital before they served Kevin's breakfast. She didn't want to risk the smell of food and coffee making her sick in front of Kevin again.

Because sleeping for any length of time in the hard recliner was impossible, she wasn't surprised when she woke up before the alarm went off. She was quietly putting on her shoes when Kevin's eyes opened.

"Hey," he said softly. "What are you doing up so early?"

"It's Saturday. I want to get to the store early, and I want to go home for a shower first."

Her answer seemed to satisfy him. He mumbled something before closing his eyes and drifting back to sleep, still under the influence of his nighttime dose of pain medication. Knowing he probably wouldn't remember their brief conversation, she wrote a note on the status board, kissed him gently, and left before the food service department began delivering breakfast trays.

An hour later, she was at home in their bathroom, staring at the pregnancy test strip. It was positive. She and Kevin were going to have a baby.

Kevin was propped up in bed sullenly picking at his lunch when

Heather got back to the hospital. "Where have you been?"

"I told you. I was at the store. It was busy and just Emily and Jacob were there, so I helped out." Heather put her purse in the small cabinet and sat down on the recliner. "It's Easter weekend. Lots of dogs and cats are going to have gourmet treats in their Easter baskets tomorrow."

"Where's Nicole? She's supposed to work on Saturdays." He was bored and frustrated. He should have been at the store this morning.

"She'll be in this afternoon. Emily's keeping both Jacob and Nicole under thirty-two hours a week."

"Oh. Right." He digested that, then said, "Emily's got to be racking up the overtime."

"I haven't checked the time sheets. I'll do that on Monday when I do the payroll. But I don't think she's working more than an hour of OT a day."

"You need to watch that. It will eat up whatever profit we might make. We don't need her taking advantage of the situation." As soon as the words were out of his mouth, he wanted to take them back.

"She's not taking advantage of anything. She's keeping the store running for us."

"I know. I'm sorry. I shouldn't have said that." He stabbed at the meat on his plate. "This is disgusting."

"You must be feeling better if you're complaining about the food. I think that's a good sign." She yawned and pushed the recliner back.

He knew he should respond to her gentle teasing with some light banter, but he didn't. "The good sign is that I walked further this morning while you were gone." He knew his words would sting.

"I'm sorry I wasn't here when you did it." Her eyes reddened and her voice trembled slightly.

"Oh, Sunshine. I'm the one who's sorry." What was wrong with him? Why was he deliberately saying things he knew would hurt her? "I'm not trying to make you feel guilty. I just want to go home. I want to be normal again. And I'm being a jerk."

"You're not a jerk. You're—" She stopped abruptly, then repeated, "You're not a jerk."

"I apologize for acting like one. If I could kick myself, I would. And I promise I'll make it up to you."

She didn't reply. Her eyes were closed. She had fallen asleep.

When Kevin opened his eyes Sunday morning, an Easter basket was on his tray table. He looked past the basket and saw Heather watching him from the recliner, obviously waiting for him to wake up. "You're amazing. How did you manage to do this?"

"The Easter Bunny did it." She sat up. "Go on. See what you got."

It was a tradition Heather had begun before they were married. On the first Easter they were together, she had given him a colorful basket with a book, a chocolate bicycle, and some muffins she had baked. She always managed to find a small but meaningful gift that she would surround with food—at least some of which they would eat for Easter breakfast.

He shook his head as he pulled the tray table closer. The small basket looked like the ones they'd purchased to make the pet supply Easter baskets for the store. It was piled high with individually wrapped baked goods that probably came from Joyful Cup. Not home baked, but obviously Heather wasn't going to let his accident stop her from at least partially keeping their traditions. "These look delicious. Will you share them with me?"

"Of course. I'll take that brownie on top."

"That's the one I wanted. But because I love you ..." As he picked up the brownie to hand it to her, he noticed something underneath. "What's this?"

"I don't know. You tell me." Heather's eyes sparkled as she suppressed a smile.

He pulled out a small infant doll. Bewildered, he stared at the toy, then shifted his gaze to Heather as comprehension dawned. "Does this mean?"

"We're going to have a real one. Of our own."

"But how?"

"Really, Kevin, do I need to explain that to you?"

"Come here." He pulled her to him, ignoring the soreness of his cracked ribs, and kissed her nose. "Get on the bed with me."

"You know that's against the rules."

"Then maybe they'll kick us of out of here for doing it. I want to hold you."

He stayed still as she pushed the tray table aside, carefully climbed onto the hospital bed and stretched out next to him. Staring into her eyes, he put his hand on her belly.

"You are the most wonderful woman in the world. And you're going to be the most wonderful mother."

"And you're going to be the most wonderful father."

Then they were both laughing and crying at the same time. Kevin kissed her tenderly on the lips. "I love you," he whispered.

"Excuse me." The voice came from the doorway as the food service worker stood there with Kevin's breakfast tray. Heather looked up, gasped, slid off the bed, and rushed to the bathroom. The sound of retching could be heard clearly from the other side of the closed door. Looking unsure, the food service worker asked, "Should I get someone?"

"No." Kevin was smiling broadly. "She's okay. You can just leave that."

Heather emerged a few minutes later, looking pale but happy. She didn't rejoin Kevin on the bed. Instead, she pushed his tray table across his lap and lifted the cover off the plate. "You should eat while it's hot."

"It won't bother you?"

"I don't think so. So far, I'm just getting sick once each morning, and then I'm done."

"How long have you known?"

"For sure? Just since yesterday. The morning sickness started on Thursday and I took the test yesterday."

"Oh, Sunshine, I—" He paused, speechless for a moment. "How far along do you think you are?"

"Five or six weeks. I've been so preoccupied that I didn't realize I was late."

"I was afraid you were coming down with something. In fact, I told Joy that when she was here. She told me not to worry."

"I think she knows." Heather adjusted his tray table and sat down in the recliner. "I was in her shop on Thursday when I got sick the first time. I think it was the smell of the coffee. She hinted that I might be pregnant, but I told her I couldn't be. Guess I was wrong."

"Do I need to explain to you how this happened?" It was Kevin's turn to tease. His thoughts flashed back briefly to the tender conversation at Thanksgiving when they decided they were ready for the children they both always wanted. "I just didn't expect you to get pregnant so quickly."

"I didn't, either. But I guess God had other plans for us."

He ignored her reference to God's plans. Did God's plan for them include being seriously injured by a hit-and-run driver? "I hate that I'm stuck in the hospital right now. We should be home together, celebrating."

"We can celebrate anywhere. And we'll be home soon. But, Kevin, let's not tell anybody yet." At his quizzical look, she explained. "At this stage, so many things can go wrong. Let's wait at least another month."

"Okay, but I want you to go to the doctor as soon as possible."

"I'll call for an appointment tomorrow. Now, eat your breakfast. I'm going to have this brownie."

"A brownie for breakfast? You're already teaching our kid some bad habits."

∽

Kevin watched Heather move briskly around the hospital room. "How are you feeling?"

"Excited. A little scared." Heather dropped her supply of toiletries in a tote bag. Kevin's discharge was official and they were just waiting for a wheelchair to take him to the car. "I'm really looking forward to having you out of here and getting you home, but I'm nervous about taking care of you by myself."

"I'm not helpless, you know. But I meant, how are you *feeling?*"

"It's going to be a long nine months if you keep asking me that every fifteen minutes." Heather scooped up a pile of cards sent by well-wishers as she continued to gather their things. "I'm fine. It seems like I just need to throw up once each morning, then everything is normal."

"Nothing is normal."

Heather stopped packing. It only took her three steps in the small room to be in front of Kevin, who was sitting up in the recliner, dressed in the clothes she had brought him to wear home. She framed his face with her hands and captured his gaze with hers.

"Our normal has changed. Our normal will never be the same as it was. Just like when we got married, our normal changed. Just like when we opened the store, our normal changed. Now we're going to have a baby, and our normal is changing again."

"A normal of me being weak and us with a mountain of debt."

"All temporary—not normal." She put an extra note of optimism in her tone to counter the anger and fear she heard in his. "Remember, the doctor said you need another month or so of healing, then you'll be able to start exercising again. You'll be back to your old self in no time. And the bills—well, we'll work that out."

"I wish I felt as positive as you."

"You'll feel better when we get you home. You just need a few sloppy Toby kisses."

"Is he at the house?"

"Not yet. He's at the store with Emily. She'll bring him home tonight." Heather kissed Kevin lightly and let her hands fall away from his face. She looked around the room. "I think I've got everything."

As if on cue, a nurse appeared at the door with a wheel-chair. It was time to face their new normal.

It was common for Samantha and Amber to carpool on the days when they had the same class schedule. Amber was waiting outside when Samantha pulled up and tapped the horn.

With a grin, Amber hopped in and fastened her seatbelt. "Whose car?"

"My grandmother's. It's been sitting for a long time. I thought it would be good to drive it." The lie Samantha had told her neighbor came easier this time. Amber didn't question it, instead launching into a discussion of everything they needed to do to be ready for their upcoming final exams. Samantha knew she had some serious catching up to do, but now that her car was safely at the bottom of Lake Jesup and she knew Kevin was recovering, she could get back to normal and focus on school.

But would life ever really be normal again?

"I never knew our house could look so good." Braced by his walker, Kevin stood in the living room, watching Heather hang her purse on the hook by the door. He'd seen her do that hundreds of times before and never paid much attention, but today he treasured those familiar motions. The last time he'd left this house, he expected to be back in a couple of hours—not almost two weeks.

Heather pulled the cord on the ceiling fan. "I guess the saving grace of not having had time to clean for the past two weeks is that no one was here to mess anything up. You sit down and I'll get the stuff out of the car."

"Wait. Stay with me for a minute. I want to hold you and not worry about someone walking in on us." Kevin reached for her, pulling her into a sweet, wordless embrace. When he finally released her, his eyes were bright with unshed tears.

Kevin knew he wouldn't be cleared to return to work for several weeks. As he watched Heather get ready for her daily trip to the store, he decided to coax her into taking him with her.

"Come on, Sunshine," he pleaded. "You know you want me to go with you. Besides, I'm going crazy in the house."

"What I want is for you to get well. You've only been out of the hospital three days. You're supposed to be resting and healing, not going to work."

"I won't work, I promise. I'll just watch you."

Heather snorted.

"So I'll go down to Joy's and get some coffee. That'll give me a short walk, I won't bother you, and I'll be out of the house."

Heather was clearly exasperated. "You are the worst patient ever. But as long as you don't do anything there that you wouldn't be doing at home, I guess it won't hurt you to go in with me."

"I'm not going to do anything stupid. I've got a pregnant wife, you know. I need to get back in shape so we can get ready for our baby."

"Just remember that." She wagged her index finger in a warning.

Kevin hadn't been away from the store for more than a few days at a time since they opened it—until now. After almost two weeks in the hospital and several days at home, he was suffering from more than simple cabin fever. He needed to reconnect with the business they had both worked so hard to build. He trusted Heather's assessment that all was going as well as could be expected, maybe even better, but he wanted to see for himself. He wasn't prepared for what he saw before they got to the store.

Heather took their usual route to the store—a route that passed the accident site. As they approached the scene, Kevin shifted in his seat and inhaled sharply. "Slow down, please."

"What?" Heather took her foot off the gas. "Oh, Kevin, I'm sorry. I wasn't thinking—"

"It's okay. I just want to look." His memory of that morning was still hazy. The doctors told him he might never recall the impact. Would seeing where it happened help him remember?

"There's really nothing to see." Heather checked the rearview mirror and began to accelerate. "I've been driving by here almost every day. It still bothers me, but not as much as it did."

"It's okay," he repeated. "Of course everything's cleaned up by now."

"And you're getting better. You survived and you're going to be okay." It had become a mantra. "We can be grateful for that."

"I guess." Being grateful it wasn't worse didn't stop him from being angry that it happened at all. But there was no reason to say that to Heather now.

They rode the rest of the way in silence. Heather parked behind the store and retrieved Kevin's walker from the trunk. He allowed her to hover—but not help—as he navigated his way through the back door and down the short hallway. There were no customers at the moment, but that wasn't unusual for mid-morning on a Friday. Surveying the store, he glanced over his shoulder at Heather. "You have no idea how good it feels to be here."

At the sound of his voice, Emily turned from the shelves

she was stocking. "Look who's here! Are you finally coming back to work, boss?"

Heather answered first. "No, he's not. He was just driving me crazy at home, so I brought him with me."

"Ah! So he could drive us crazy here?"

"Actually, no. He's going to go get some coffee and give Joy the pleasure of his company," Heather said pointedly.

Kevin rolled his eyes. "Stop talking about me like I'm not here. I'll be back soon, Emily. The store looks great. Whose idea was it to set up those displays?"

"Aren't they wonderful?" Emily gushed. "It's the coolest thing. One of the customers did them. Her name is Samantha Lawrence."

"A customer?"

"She came in when we were doing the last adoption event. It was crazy busy, and I was tripping over canned food cases. She just started stocking the shelves and straightening things up. Then a few days later, she came back in. I was setting up the dish display and she offered to do it. She did a beautiful job. Then she arranged the Easter baskets. She's come by a few times since then and helps out for a while. She'll do anything—the displays, stocking, sweeping. She says her grandmother really liked you, so she wanted to help out."

"Who was her grandmother?"

"She told me, but I don't—"

"Linda Kenyon," Heather said. "Remember the lady who had a cat and lived in the townhouses across the street? You used to tell her she needed to get more cats. Her granddaughter came in a while back to tell us that she had died."

"I tell everybody to get more pets. That way they'll buy more stuff from us." Kevin remembered Linda Kenyon but was hazy on her granddaughter. "What did you say the granddaughter's name was? Samantha? Maybe we can hire her to come in a few times a month to do the displays, after we get back to normal operations."

"Maybe." Heather raised her eyebrows. "Don't you have someplace to go?"

"Right." Kevin shifted on his walker and turned toward the back of the store. "Just as soon as I check out the office."

Heather blocked him. "No. No work for you, remember? So no office."

"You're cruel." He kissed her nose and changed directions. The walker clattered as he made his way to the front door. "I'll be at Joy's if anybody needs me."

When Joy saw Kevin, her face broke into a big smile and she rushed out from behind the counter to give Kevin a gentle hug. "It's good to see you. But what are you doing here?"

"Heather kicked me out of the store."

"What were you doing in the store? Should you even be out of the house?"

"Probably not." Kevin shrugged. "But I've been cooped up too long."

"I know this is frustrating for you because you're used to being active, but—"

"Don't say it," he interrupted. "I hear it enough from Heather. I'm getting plenty of rest."

Joy laughed. "I'm sure you are. What would you like? Have a seat and I'll bring it to you."

"Don't treat me like an invalid." He didn't want to admit that he was getting tired and needed to sit down, or that he would have trouble carrying his coffee to a table while using a walker.

"I'm treating you like the friend and special customer that you are." She guided him to a table at the back of the shop where he could relax away from the main traffic of the shop. "I'll get you some coffee."

A few minutes later, she placed two steaming mugs on the table and settled into the chair across from him without waiting for an invitation.

"Would you like to join me?" He smirked as he made the offer.

"I thought you'd never ask. Now, tell me how things are going. Heather hasn't been in since you got out of the hospital. How is she?"

"She's fine." He picked up his sturdy brown cup with a military seal on it. "She's overdoing it, of course."

"Well, under the circumstances, that's to be expected. Is she still getting sick in the morning?"

Kevin hesitated. He and Heather had agreed not to tell anyone about the baby yet, but Heather thought Joy at least suspected. Should he say anything?

"It's okay. Don't tell me." Joy reached across the table and squeezed his hand. "I'm happy for you. So tell me how you're doing. How much longer before you can get back to work?"

"At least a few more weeks. I have to use the walker. I can't lift anything. Can't drive. But I got my bike back."

"Really? Can you fix it?"

"No. It's beyond fixing. I'll have to get a new one. But I wanted to keep it. I like to look at it and think about what I'd do to the piece of garbage who hit me." At the expression on her face, he softened his tone and backtracked. "Not really. I've just had that bike for a long time. I was attached to it."

Joy sighed. "It's understandable that you're angry. But getting revenge isn't going to change anything."

"I know. It's not that I want revenge, I want justice. I want—" He stopped. What did he want?

"You want for this to not have happened."

"Yeah. You're a smart lady. Have you figured out how to turn back time? So I can go back and not ride that morning?"

"I wish." She stared into her light green cup for a moment, then met his gaze. "The best I can do is encourage you to forgive the person."

"Oh, I have." He knew how insincere the words sounded as soon as he said them. An explanation would help. "I talked a lot about it with our pastor while I was in the hospital. And Heather and I have even prayed for him."

"That's good. It's part of the process. You've been seriously hurt, Kevin, and it seems like you're healing physically. But you need to heal your heart as well as your body. And for that to happen, you have to be honest with yourself."

"I'm being honest." He hoped he didn't sound as defensive as he felt.

"Really?" Her tone was gentle but direct. "You've forgiven someone you just called a piece of garbage?"

Kevin drew in a breath to speak, then stopped. Joy was looking around the room. He appreciated the lack of eye contact. It gave him some time to consider his response. Finally he said the only thing he could think of—even though it sounded weak to his own ears. "I want to forgive him."

Joy returned her gaze to his. "That's a good first step. You know, for most of us, forgiveness—especially for something as major as what happened to you—takes time. And effort. We don't simply decide to forgive someone and poof! It just happens. We make the choice to forgive and then we work on it. We pray about it. We find a way to make peace with it. We figure out how God can take what happened and use it for good."

"You just lost me. What good can possibly come of this?"

"If I could tell you God's plan, I would. But I'm not God and I don't have all the answers. Still, I've seen some good already. The support from people in your church. The support from the community."

"That's God using me being injured for good?"

"You tell me."

"I think it's people stepping up to take care of Heather and me when God let us down." As soon as the words were out, Kevin regretted them. Joy was just trying to help and he'd given her a verbal slap in the face. Except she didn't flinch.

"Oh, Kevin, God didn't let you down. God never lets us down."

"I'd like to believe that, Joy. I really would. In fact, I thought I did. But right now, I don't." Gripping his walker, he got carefully to his feet. "Why did God let this happen? Can you answer that?"

"No, I can't. But I think God smiles a little when we ask that question because it acknowledges his power." Joy stood and picked up their mugs.

Kevin snorted as he pulled his wallet from his pocket and dropped a few dollars onto the table. "How do you do it? I always thought redheads were supposed to be hot-tempered. But you—you're always so calm and even-tempered. Even when people like me are trying to provoke you."

"I got my hair and my temperament from my father. He taught me not to waste my energy on things I can't control. And I don't think you're trying to provoke me. You're being honest about your feelings, and that's a good thing."

"If you say so." He shifted on his walker and took a step. "I've got to go. Heather should be finished with what she needed to do, so we can go home. Thanks for the company."

He felt her watching him as he made his way out the door.

Kevin had been out of the hospital just over a week and was gaining strength daily. Though not officially cleared by his doctors, he had convinced Heather to let him work a few hours. With Toby dozing at his feet, he was in the store's small office reviewing the summer promotion schedule.

Emily appeared in the doorway. With a broad smile on her face, she spoke in a whisper. "Kevin, can you take a break? There's someone here I think you'll want to see."

"Be right there." He made a few notes then braced himself on his walker. The motion alerted Toby, who followed Kevin and Emily to the front of the store where a young woman was rearranging merchandise on the shelves near the door.

"Surprise!" Emily's voice returned to normal volume. As the young woman turned, Emily added, "Samantha, look who's finally back at work. Kevin, this is our display angel."

"Ah! The wonderful Samantha." Kevin held out his hand. "I hear we have a lot to thank you for."

"Uh, no." Samantha blinked several times as she reached to return his handshake, then clarified. "I don't know about wonderful, I just wanted to help out. There's nothing to thank me for."

Kevin got the distinct impression that she was uncomfortable. How could she find him intimidating? "I don't think you're taking enough credit. Emily said you were a lifesaver the weekend after my accident. And your displays are better than anything we've ever done ourselves. We need to put you on the payroll."

Samantha shook her head and stammered slightly. "I don't—I don't need to be paid. Um, so you're doing okay?"

"Still not fully recovered, but I'm getting there."

"That's good. I'm glad to hear it." Samantha was looking everywhere but at him.

"I'm sorry my wife isn't here at the moment. She's out running errands, but I know she'd love to see you and thank you, too."

"Really. That's not necessary. I like doing this. It's not a big deal." Was there a hint of panic in her voice?

"It may not be a big deal to you, but it is to us." Kevin decided a change of subject might help Samantha relax. "You know, we still miss your grandmother. She was one of my favorite customers."

"She liked you, too." Samantha fidgeted with one of the books on dog training she had been arranging on display stands.

"When she would come in, she used to talk about you and how much she enjoyed having you living with her."

"Thanks." Samantha placed the book in a display rack and immediately picked it up again. "We were close."

"Well." Kevin wasn't sure what else to say. To give himself a moment to think, he scratched Toby's head. He couldn't think of anything else, so he returned to the topic of the displays Samantha had created. "We really do appreciate what you've done. It's going to be a while before I'm back full-time and we can go back to our regular store hours, so I'm not in a position to offer you a job right now. But maybe at some point you would be interested in a part-time job doing our displays."

"I don't know. I stay pretty busy with school."

"But you found time to help us. That says a lot about you.

Your grandmother would be proud."

Samantha turned her head away, but not before Kevin saw her eyes brighten with tears. He felt like kicking himself.

"I'm sorry. I didn't mean to upset you."

"You didn't." She faced him with a smile that seemed forced. "I'll just take care of these shelves, then I have to go."

Kevin was at a loss for words. He felt as awkward as he thought she was, but he wasn't sure why. "Well, thank you again. It was great seeing you."

A caffe mocha and a large chocolate cupcake.

After making her escape from Wyland's, Samantha ended up at Joyful Cup ordering comfort food. Emily must think she's crazy, coming in to work on the displays then leaving right after talking to Kevin. And she didn't want to think about what Kevin probably thought of her, barely able to speak and almost crying.

The wonderful Samantha.

Your grandmother would be proud.

Kevin had no idea how wrong he was. What would he say if he knew who she really was, that she had hit him and left him on the side of the road, not knowing if he was alive or dead, doing nothing to help him? That she only started going to his store to find out how he was doing, not because she had any intention of doing volunteer work there? That she only continued volunteering so she could get more information?

Samantha found a table in the back of Joyful Cup where she would have some privacy. As she contemplated the rich confection she hoped would make her feel better, her appetite disappeared. She propped her elbows on the table and rested her head in her hands.

"That looks yummy. Are you rewarding yourself?"

At the sound of Joy's voice, Samantha's head snapped up.

"No, not really. It just looked so good."

"It's rich. I usually recommend sharing those cupcakes." Without asking permission, Joy dropped into the chair across from Samantha. "Something on your mind?"

"Just the usual. School. Finals." The answer was true, if not complete.

"And missing your grandmother. She would have enjoyed half of that."

"She would have eaten more than half." Samantha smiled, thinking about the times when she and Gram would share one of Joyful Cup's delicious treats. "She was a chocoholic from way back. She could give you a long list of reasons why chocolate is good for you."

"And every one of them would be right. But you're not eating."

"Yeah, Gram knew her stuff." Samantha couldn't meet Joy's gaze. She picked up her fork and took a small bite of frosting.

"She was a wise woman. It must be hard for you, with her being gone and you not having any other family here."

"I have friends. And my mom and I talk."

"But it's not the same. Grandmothers are special. I hope I'm not out of line by saying this. I think there's something going on that you would like to be able to talk to your grandmother about."

Samantha stared at the cupcake. She thought about taking another bite, but wasn't sure she could swallow it. Joy was silent. It was a technique Gram used—she'd say something that wasn't quite a question but needed a response, then she'd be quiet until the other person spoke. The approach always garnered unsolicited confessions of misdeeds from Samantha and her cousins when they were growing up. But those childish transgressions were nothing compared to what Samantha was hiding now.

"There's always something I'd like to tell her." Samantha

was surprised at the light tone she managed. "I talk to her cat instead."

"Cats are good listeners, but they're not very good at giving advice."

"True." Samantha put her fork down. She had escaped from Wyland's, now she wanted to escape from Joyful Cup. "Could I get a box for this? I think I'll take it home and eat it later."

"Of course. Do you want a to-go cup for your coffee?"

"No, thanks." Samantha took a long drink of the now-tepid café mocha, watching as Joy went behind the counter and returned with a small box. Instead of just leaving the box on the table, Joy sat back down.

"I know I'm not your grandmother, but I considered her a friend and I consider you a friend. I want you to know I'm here if you need to talk. Anything you say stays between us. I promise."

Samantha wondered if Joy could really keep that promise if she told the truth, that she had committed a serious crime. She couldn't take the chance. Besides, what would telling anyone accomplish? It wouldn't change anything and would only increase the chances she'd be caught. Kevin was going to be okay. Her car was at the bottom of a lake. She just had to get on with her life.

Heather returned from her errands and promptly sent Kevin out for coffee. "This office isn't big enough for both of us. Go take a break. I need about an hour and then we can go home."

"I'd argue with you, but I have to admit, I'm tired. Text me when you're ready." Kevin clipped his phone to his belt and grabbed his walker.

As he approached Joyful Cup, he saw Samantha come out

and walk briskly in the other direction. He started to call out but stopped when he remembered how ill-at-ease she had been earlier. Slowing his pace, he watched her cross the parking lot to the traffic light, where she pressed the signal button and waited. Did she honestly not realize how much help she'd been to them? Though it wasn't a lot in terms of hours, it was substantial in terms of benefits—keeping the shelves stocked, creating attractive displays that boosted sales. He and Heather would have to come up with a way to express their appreciation that she would accept. The light changed. Samantha crossed the street and disappeared from his line of vision. Shaking his head, he continued to Joyful Cup.

Joy looked up from straightening the magazine rack when Kevin entered the shop. "Kicked out again?" she asked cheerfully.

"You don't need to sound so happy about it." Gripping his walker, he made his way to one of the bistro tables by the window. "The office isn't big enough for more than one person and she won't let me work in the store because she's afraid I'll lift something I shouldn't."

"Your wife is a smart lady. Sit down. What can I get you?"

"Black coffee, thanks. Did I see Samantha Lawrence leave here?"

"A few minutes ago, yes. Why do you ask?"

"Since the crash, she's been coming into the store, helping Emily while Heather and I were out. I saw her in the store a little while ago and we talked for a few minutes." He debated on whether to say anything about how odd he found it that she had apparently come by to spend some time in the store, then suddenly had to leave, but had time to stop at Joy's.

"She was at your store?"

"Yes, helping with the displays. Emily had the impression that she was planning to be there for a while but when I came out to meet her, she seemed to get nervous and then she left."

Joy's brows knitted slightly, but her tone was light. "She must have been overwhelmed by your charm. I'll get your coffee."

A moment later, she set a white mug with black letters on the table and sat down across from him. "So how are things going? How does it feel to be back at work?"

He pulled the mug toward him and chuckled as he read the slogan on it: *I'm trying to be awesome today, but I'm exhausted from being so freakin' awesome yesterday.* "I like that. How does it feel to be back at work? Good and frustrating. Good because I was going crazy at home. Frustrating because I can't do everything I want to do and I get tired."

"That's part of the healing process."

"I know. But we need to get the store back to normal operating hours. For that to happen, Heather and I need to be working full-time."

"It's only been a few weeks, Kevin. You need to be patient."

"I don't have time to be patient." Kevin sighed, shaking his head. "Okay, I know how stupid that sounded. But the hospital bills are going to start coming in soon and there are other things." Like a baby, but he didn't want to mention that.

"And how is being impatient and frustrated going to help with any of that?" Joy asked mildly.

"Don't you ever get tired of being so calm and reasonable?"

"It's my job. I sell coffee with a side of calm. It counteracts the caffeine."

They were both laughing when Sergeant Grant walked in. He raised his hand in greeting and strode to the counter, where the barista took his order.

"Good afternoon, Sergeant," Joy called to him. "Are you meeting someone or would you like to join us?" She stood and pulled an empty chair over from the next table.

Kevin struggled to his feet and held out his hand. "Good to see you again." At the officer's quizzical expression, he added, "Kevin Wyland. You're investigating my accident."

"Mr. Wyland. Right. I'm sorry I didn't recognize you. Please sit down. You're looking much better than you were the last time I saw you. How are you doing?" Sergeant Grant rested his hand on the back of the seat Joy offered.

"Today I'm getting a lecture in patience from Joy." Kevin carefully lowered himself into his chair. "A few days ago it was a lecture on how I need to forgive the delightful person who hit me and left me on the side of the road."

Joy rolled her eyes. "I don't lecture and you know it. I just tell the truth."

The sergeant put his cup on the table and settled into his seat. "Well, I wish I had some news about the 'delightful person who hit' you, but I don't."

"Still no leads?"

"I'm sorry. We're still waiting for the lab to get back with us on the debris we recovered at the scene, but that may not be much help. No reports from body shops, no calls to Crimeline. We don't have a lot to go on."

"I can't believe they're going to get away with this." Kevin didn't try to hide his anger.

"They haven't gotten away with it yet. We haven't closed the investigation."

"Is there anything I can do?"

"No. We'll keep working on it." The sergeant sipped his coffee.

"I'm curious. If you do find the driver, what will happen to him?" Kevin's experience with law enforcement and the judicial system had been limited to a few traffic citations when he was a teenager.

"He—or she—is facing some serious charges. I'm guessing they'd strike a plea deal. The sentence will depend on a lot of things—his criminal history, whether or not he was impaired, other things. At the least, he'll probably get his license suspended and get probation. He could go to jail. And that's too bad, because if he had stopped, there might not have been any charges. Or, assuming he wasn't drunk, maybe just a ticket for careless driving."

Kevin drummed on the table while he processed the information. "I understand that arresting the guy isn't going to change what happened, but I guess I just want to see him be held accountable."

Then Sergeant Grant answered a question Kevin had been reluctant to ask. "You're right—arresting the driver won't change what happened, but it could make a difference to you. If he gets a plea, the deal could include restitution for damages—the cost of your bike and your medical expenses. And you might have a civil case against him. Of course, he'd have to have insurance and some assets to make suing him worthwhile. I'm not a lawyer but if we do make an arrest, you may want to talk to one."

As Kevin digested the advice, his phone buzzed with a text. Glancing at it, he said, "That's Heather. She's ready to go. Sergeant, thanks for everything. And, Joy, thanks for the truth."

"You know I'm here whenever you need someone to talk to."

"I know." But he wasn't thinking about talking. He was thinking that finding the hit-and-run driver could solve their financial problems. But how could he help make that happen?

Kevin logged out of the accounting program. He'd been coming into the store a few hours a day for a week now, working mostly in the office but occasionally greeting customers. Though he was still using a walker to move more than a few steps, his stamina was improving, and he thought he would be ready to cut back on his pain medication soon. Equally important was that the store was doing okay. Sales were holding steady, despite the shortened hours. All of the business bills were current, and there was enough cash to meet payroll, even with Emily's over-time. Of course, none of the hospital or doctor bills had come in yet and he had no idea how they were going to pay them when they did, but at least the store was solvent.

He could hear voices from the front of the store. Emily was working the counter and helping customers. Heather was cleaning, something she usually did when the store was closed, but they weren't coming early or staying late these days. She was still suffering from morning sickness. Once the first bout of nausea passed, she was fine for the rest of the day, so they had been waiting for that before going out in the morning. By evening, they were both too tired to work.

Using his walker, he made his way around the sales counter, greeting the customers and watching Heather. It was so typical of her to take on the less desirable jobs and get them done instead of delegating them to employees.

"Are you okay?" She looked over her shoulder at him as she wiped a shelf with a dust cloth.

"Just a little tired. I've been working hard." His joke seemed flat as he realized he was breathing faster than usual.

"Give me five minutes to finish up and we'll go home."

He wanted to tell her to take her time, but suddenly everything in the room seemed far away. And then he felt a sharp pain in his chest. He gasped, gripping his walker.

"Kevin! What's wrong?" Heather was at his side, one arm across his shoulders, the other hand on his arm.

He could barely speak. "Chest. Hurts. Can't breathe."

Someone—maybe Emily or one of the customers—pushed a chair behind him and helped Heather lower him onto it. He heard someone say, "I'm calling 911." Then Heather was kneeling in front of him, her hands on his cheeks.

"Kevin, look at me. Can you hear me?"

He nodded, not wanting to say anything. Each shallow pant was a stabbing pain in his chest, and words would require more breath. Was he having a heart attack?

"It's okay. You're okay. Don't try to talk. Just focus on me."

Her steady gaze held his panic at bay. She continued to speak softly, almost chanting, that he was okay, everything would be okay, help was on the way.

Minutes later, he heard the siren and then paramedics were in the store. It was organized chaos as they moved swiftly and efficiently through their routine. In minutes, Kevin was on a gurney being wheeled to the ambulance, with Heather walking alongside, holding his hand. He heard one of the paramedics explain that she couldn't ride with them.

Squeezing his hand, she brushed his cheek with her lips. "I'll meet you at the hospital." She stepped back as they lifted him into the vehicle.

The doors slammed and he closed his eyes. Would he even

make it to the hospital?

~

The table was a mess, with dirty plates, empty cups, and wadded up paper napkins scattered amid books and folders. Samantha had been in Joyful Cup for nearly three hours, drinking coffee and snacking as she worked. Eyes riveted to her computer screen, she gave her paper a final review. Finally she sat back, closed her laptop, and stretched. The paper probably could have been better, but considering all that had happened over the last few weeks, it was good enough. If she could just get through next week's final exams, she'd be able to take a break, put the accident behind her, and get back on track in the new semester.

As she stood up and began stacking the dishes, Joy appeared at her side. "Let me take those. Looks like you've been working hard."

"Yes, but I'm done. I didn't realize you were here."

"I just got back. Want to join me for a cappuccino? I need a break. You could probably use one, too."

Samantha packed up her books and laptop, moving them off the table onto a chair. She was placing her backpack on the floor as Joy returned with two foam-topped mugs.

"I probably don't need any more caffeine," Samantha said as she accepted the white ribbed mug monogrammed with a K.

"How long have you been here?" Joy grabbed a few napkins from the supply bar.

"Long enough to eat a brownie and a muffin, drink a latte and at least three cups of plain coffee."

"I'm surprised you're not walking on the ceiling. Want me to remake that with decaf?"

"No, thanks. I've still got plenty of studying to do." Samantha pointed to her books. "So you're having a rough day?"

"More like long and exhausting. You know Kevin and

Heather Wyland? Kevin's in the hospital."

Joy's words came like a punch in the stomach to Samantha. "What happened?"

"He was in the store this morning and had chest pains. They took him to the hospital in an ambulance. I drove Heather to the hospital and sat with her while they ran tests."

"Was it a heart attack?" Samantha carefully placed her mug on the table and dropped her hands in her lap. If she started trembling, she didn't want Joy to see it.

"They aren't sure."

"Is he going to be okay?" That was a dumb question. How could Joy know?

"He was awake and alert when I left, and I think that's a good sign. We'll find out more tomorrow." Joy leaned back with a sigh, sipping her cappuccino from a dark blue mug with part of Psalm 73:26 in white letters: *God is the strength of my heart.*

Samantha's mind was racing. Could this be related to the accident? "I saw him last week. He was using a walker but he seemed to be doing okay."

"Well, he had some serious injuries. From the little bit I overheard at the hospital, this could be a complication from those injuries or it could be something totally separate. We'll just have to wait to find out."

"I know. I just—" Samantha paused, trying to tamp down her fears. She had thought that if Kevin recovered completely, the police might not try as hard to find out who hit him. But this could move the crash up on the investigator's priority list. Of course, she had no idea how police actually prioritized their work. Right now, that didn't matter. What mattered was that she had to get herself under control so Joy wouldn't wonder what was wrong. "It just doesn't seem fair, that's all."

"No, it's not fair. Kevin and Heather are good people and they don't deserve this. But accidents happen."

"You believe it was an accident?"

"Of course I do. I'm sure that driver didn't hit Kevin on purpose."

"But he should have stopped." Why did she say that? She didn't want to talk with Joy about the driver—or did she?

"Yes, he should have stopped. But that's a separate issue from the accident itself."

"Would it have made a difference to Kevin?" Samantha had wondered this since the day she found out who she'd hit. Would Joy have the answer?

"From what I know, I don't think so. At least not from a physical perspective. The witness who saw the crash called 911 right away. Kevin's injuries wouldn't have been any different and he wouldn't have gotten to the hospital any faster if the driver had stopped."

"So you don't think the person who did this to Kevin is evil?" It was as much a plea for reassurance as it was a question.

"No. I think the person made a mistake. And it was a serious mistake." Joy leaned toward Samantha. "But this wasn't evil. Sometimes good people do bad things. Those bad things might be calculated and intentional, or they might be unplanned and impulsive—they might be an accident. The thing is, evil people don't feel guilt or shame for what they do. They take pleasure in it. I don't think that's what happened. I think the driver who hit Kevin is feeling a lot of guilt and shame—and probably regret for not stopping."

"But I've heard some people say some ugly things—calling the driver a monster, scum of the earth, and worse. Saying they'd like to hurt him the way he hurt Kevin." Below the table, Samantha's hands clinched into fists, her nails digging into her palms.

"Sometimes people say things they don't really mean when they're upset." Joy took a deep breath, appearing to consider her words carefully. "Look, the first thing you need to remember is that these are all people who don't know the driver. They don't know anything about this person other than that he caused an accident and drove away. They're making their entire judgment of this person based on a single moment, a single decision. Just like you said that it's not fair that this happened to Kevin, it's not fair to make judgments like that. But it's human and understandable. Second, some people are angry on Kevin's behalf and they express that anger by saying ugly things. Don't let it bother you."

Samantha stared into her cup, avoiding Joy's eyes as she tried to come up with a response. Was Joy wondering why she was so bothered by what others thought of the hit-and-run driver? She wanted desperately to tell someone what she'd done, but she couldn't.

After a moment, Joy laughed softly. "This certainly is a depressing conversation. It wasn't what I had in mind. Let's change the subject. Tell me about your tattoo."

"My tattoo?" Samantha didn't try to hide her surprise, even though she knew her sleeveless top revealed the phases of the moon that made a trail on her inner right arm from below her armpit to above her elbow.

Joy's shoulders lifted in a small shrug. "I'm always curious about why people choose the particular tattoos they do. I thought it might be something you'd enjoy talking about. I hope you don't mind me asking."

"No, of course not." Samantha looked down at her arm and thought back to the day she chose this design. "I've always liked the moon. It's mysterious and predictable at the same time. There's something magic about it and yet you know you can count on it going through its cycle. Do you know the moon's cycle is twenty-nine and a half days? Most people think it's twenty-eight, but that's how long it takes for the moon to complete an orbit around the earth. To go through a cycle of phases from new moon to new moon takes twenty-nine and a half days."

"I don't think I knew that."

"It's true. You can see it on the calendar. I like being re-minded that some things are constant."

"I like the moon, too. It's beautiful in every phase. Like you say, you can count on it going through its cycle. I think another message we get from the moon is one of hope. No matter what happens, we always start over with a new moon. It's a promise of fresh starts."

"Fresh starts. That's good. I could use a fresh start." It was an opening to tell Joy what she'd done, that she was the horrible person who hit Kevin and drove away. But then what? Joy would probably call the police. Samantha wanted a fresh start—but she didn't want to have to go to jail to get it.

"Kevin, talk to me. Please." Heather couldn't stand Kevin's silence any longer.

He had been lying still since the cardiologist left the hospital room, staring at the ceiling. Without looking at her, he said flatly, "What's there to talk about?"

Standing next to his bed, Heather searched for an answer. "We can talk about how you feel. About how we're going to deal with this."

"The doctor told us how we're going to deal with this. How I feel doesn't matter."

Heather was doing her best to hold back tears. She wasn't sure if the desire to cry was stemming from relief that Kevin hadn't had a heart attack, fear about what the actual diagnosis of a pulmonary embolism meant, or just pregnancy hormones. Probably a combination of all three. At least Kevin was responding to her now. She wanted to keep him talking. "Do you have any questions about what the doctor said? I could look it up."

"I thought she explained it clearly." He was stone-faced, still not looking at her, and speaking robotically. "I have a blood clot in one of the pulmonary arteries in my lungs. She's going to treat it with blood thinners. I'll be in the hospital for another day or so. It will take a while for the clot to completely dissolve. While that's happening, I can expect to feel short of breath and

I'll get tired easily. Most people recover from a pulmonary embolism and lead normal lives."

"Exactly." Heather tried to sound positive and cheerful. "You'll be fine by the time the baby gets here."

"She also said that I'll need to be on blood thinners for up to a year. And that I could still develop pulmonary hypertension." Kevin turned his head away from Heather, his voice still emotionless. "That means I'll never be able to exercise again. I won't be able to teach my child to ride a bike or to play sports with him."

"But she didn't say that's what would happen She said it was the worst case scenario." When the doctor explained Kevin's prognosis, Heather kept her focus optimistic. In a sharp contrast, Kevin was totally pessimistic, almost badgering the doctor as he demanded to know the most negative possible outcome.

Kevin turned his head so he could look at Heather. "Worst case is what we've been getting lately, isn't it? Or do you call getting hit by a hit-and-run driver a good thing?"

Heather's patience snapped. "I call surviving the accident a good thing. I call all the help we've been getting from friends and even people we don't know a good thing. I call our baby a good thing. No, being a hit-and-run victim wasn't a good thing, but it happened and we have to deal with it." She realized she was sobbing, but the words kept tumbling out. "This didn't just happen to *you*, Kevin. It happened to *us*. To you, to me, to our baby, to the people who care about us. And this—this pulmonary embolism thing, it's another bump in the road. But I think we can get past it. I always thought there was nothing in this world that you and I couldn't handle together. Are you telling me I was wrong?"

They stared at each other for a long moment. Heather turned in search of a tissue, blowing her nose and wiping her eyes before turning back to Kevin. She saw a range of emotions flicker across his face before his expression went blank.

"I'm sorry," he said flatly. "I'd like to be alone for a while, if you don't mind."

Tears welled up again. Heather's throat thickened. Not sure if she could speak, she stared at him, unable to believe she had heard him correctly.

Closing his eyes, he repeated softly, "Please. I need to be alone."

Hot tears slipped down Heather's cheek. Without a word, she grabbed her purse and walked stiffly out of the room.

Afternoons were usually slow at Joyful Cup. Only a few customers occupied the tables and Molly was behind the counter when Samantha came through the door, warm from the walk over. Mid-April in Florida meant afternoon highs in the eighties. Samantha ordered an iced vanilla chai tea and tapped her credit card on the payment terminal. "Is Joy here?"

"She's in the back. Want me to get her?" Molly scooped ice into a tall glass and filled it with the rich cold brew.

"Um, no. Don't bother her." Samantha picked up her tea and headed to one of the tables in the back, away from the other customers. Joy never stayed out of sight of the customers for long. She'd be out on her own soon enough.

Fear and guilt were eating away at Samantha. What was she afraid of? It didn't make sense. The only evidence linking her to the crash was safely at the bottom of Lake Jesup. Even if the car were found, they couldn't prove she was driving it. Still, every time she saw a police officer, her muscles tensed and her pulse raced. If she had been looking at the road instead of texting Amber, she wouldn't have hit Kevin. But she couldn't change what happened. She had done her best to make up for it by helping out in the Wylands' store and sharing the fundraising page. How could she put this behind her and move on with her life?

She desperately needed to talk about it, but she didn't dare tell anyone the whole story. If only she could figure out a way to share at least part of it. That might help relieve some of her anxiety.

Sipping her tea, Samantha watched the door behind the counter that led to the shop's small office, willing Joy to come out. Finally the door opened. She summoned the self-control she needed to remain seated, to look like she was just casually enjoying a cool drink on a warm day.

Joy spoke to Molly then came around the counter. "No computer? No books?"

"I'm taking a break."

"That's what I'm doing." With a sigh, Joy slid into the chair opposite Samantha. "I love everything about this business except the paperwork."

"Is there a lot of it?"

"More than I'd prefer. I'd love to just serve folks coffee, tea and muffins and not have to worry about keeping track of money or taxes or insurance. But that's not life in this world." Joy glanced around the shop then met Samantha's gaze. "So finals are next week, right? Do you have a lot of studying to do?"

"More than I'd prefer." Samantha grinned as she mimicked Joy.

"I have faith in you. You'll get it done."

"Yeah." It was the opening Samantha hoped for. "It's just been hard to concentrate."

"Oh?"

"I've had something on my mind." Ice rattled as Samantha shook her glass.

Joy reached across the table to pat Samantha's arm. "I bet

you miss having your grandmother to talk to."

"I do. But I don't think I could talk to her about this."

"Well, I'm a pretty good listener."

"The thing is, I can't tell anyone."

"I certainly wouldn't want you to betray any confidences."

Samantha tilted her head. What was Joy trying to say? After a moment, feeling like a child trying to hide the truth from her parent, she spoke cautiously. "A friend of mine did something wrong. Something serious. And she's feeling ashamed and guilty. I don't know how to help her."

"If she's feeling guilty, that's a good thing."

"It is?" What could possibly be good about this guilt that was threatening to overwhelm her, that interrupted her sleep with nightmares, that made her feel sick during the day?

Joy leaned back, put her hands together and made a steeple with her fingertips. "Let me explain. When people feel ashamed, they're focusing on themselves. They regret what they did but all they're doing is beating themselves up. Shame and embarrassment go together. And most people try to deal with shame by keeping it a secret. Their first choice is to keep people from finding out about whatever they did."

"That makes sense. But keeping secrets is not always easy to do." If Samantha were caught and arrested, it would be public knowledge—there would be no way she would be able to prevent everyone from knowing.

"No, it's not. Especially with today's technology. But that's not my point." Joy tapped her fingertips together before her hands resumed the steeple position. "What's important to understand is that guilt and shame are different. I'm talking about the emotion of guilt, not guilt in a legal sense. When people feel shame, they want to hide. When they feel guilty about something, they usually want to fix the situation. They focus on the person they harmed. They want to correct their mistake. You can certainly feel guilt and shame at the same time, but guilt can help you take responsibility for your mistakes and try to make them right."

"I never thought of it that way." Samantha chewed on her lower lip. "But what my friend did is something she can't fix. It can't be fixed."

"That's tough." The door to the shop opened. Joy watched as the customer approached the counter and was greeted by Molly, then returned her attention to Samantha. "When you make a mistake, of course the best thing is to correct it. Sometimes that's possible, sometimes it isn't. And when it isn't, it's time to work on forgiveness."

"Forgiveness? She doesn't need to forgive anyone. She hurt people. She needs forgiveness."

"Exactly. If she's feeling guilt and shame, she needs to forgive herself." Joy stood. "I'm sorry. Looks like Molly needs some help. I'll be back in a minute."

Samantha barely heard her. She had wondered if Kevin could ever forgive her, if her parents would forgive her if they found out. But forgive herself? How?

Joy came back carrying a cup of hot tea for herself and a maroon plate of mini-cookies. "I could use a sugar fix. How about you?"

Samantha doubted that she could taste anything but she took one of the bite-sized morsels to be polite. She tried to find a smooth way to resume the conversation about forgiveness, but nothing came to mind so she just jumped in. "I'll tell my friend what you said about forgiving herself."

"I hope it helps her. Most people find it harder to forgive themselves than to forgive others. Probably because we expect more from ourselves."

"Probably." Samantha murmured agreement. "So, how do people do it? Forgive themselves?"

"I start with prayer."

"You?" Samantha was incredulous. "I can't picture you ever doing anything you need to forgive yourself for."

"I'm human, Samantha. I make mistakes, just like everyone else. I need forgiveness, just like everyone else." After a brief pause, Joy continued. "I ask God to help me let go of the guilt and shame, to show me a way I can make amends."

"I don't know if my friend believes in God." Samantha rarely thought much about God. Though Gram's faith had been strong, her parents were casual about religion and had raised her to be the same.

"You don't have to believe in God to pray."

That didn't make sense to Samantha. "Then who would you be praying to?"

"To God, of course. I know that sounds confusing. But God hears our prayers even when we don't realize we're praying. And He will answer prayers even from people who doubt Him."

"I've never heard that before."

"I'm not surprised, but I bet you've experienced it. Samantha, there are some things we just can't do on our own. We need help." When the door to the shop opened again, Joy looked away from Samantha and waved at the middle-aged man who entered.

"Hey, I was hoping you'd be here," the man boomed as he headed to their table.

"What can I do for you, Jason?" Joy got to her feet.

"I need to order coffee and pastries for a staff meeting tomorrow."

"Molly can help you with that." As Joy walked toward the counter, he followed.

"I've got something else. Shannon's been following the news about Kevin Wyland. She wants to do something for him."

"That's very kind of her. Do you know there's a HelpNow account? She can make a contribution to that. I've got the link here on a flyer."

Samantha was grateful for the interruption. It gave her some time to contemplate what Joy had said. In just a few minutes, Joy was back with two glasses of water.

"Where were we?" Joy chewed thoughtfully on one of the small cookies. "I know we've been talking about your friend, but let me ask you this: Have you ever in your mind and heart asked for help when you weren't really thinking about who you were asking?"

"I guess so." Especially lately. "But I didn't consider it prayer."

"We'll come back to that. Here's another question: Have you ever felt thankful for something good, even if you were expecting whatever it was but especially if it was a surprise?"

"Sure."

"Who were those thoughts directed to? Who were you asking for help? Who were you thanking?"

"I don't know. I didn't think about it."

"Those were prayers. And God heard them." Joy sipped her water. "Whether or not your friend believes in God isn't important right now. God believes in her. That's what matters."

Samantha's eyes narrowed with skepticism. "God believes in us?"

"Of course. Faith is a two-way street." The middle-aged man was leaving. Joy waved at him. "Now, when something I've done is eating me, especially if it's making me feel unlovable, I pray for God to take away all my negative feelings, to help me stop condemning myself. Then I ask for guidance in making things right. Sometimes that might be as simple as an apology. Sometimes it's more complicated. Or there might not be anything I can do, and then I just have to accept it."

"Accepting that you can't fix it? That's hard."

"Hard, yes, but it's actually simple. Just own it, stop the excuses, and take responsibility. Then make the conscious choice to forgive yourself."

"Well, my friend knows what she did. She's not denying it."

"Acknowledging our actions and taking responsibility for them are two different things." Joy picked up another cookie, then put it down. "I don't need any more of those. You eat the rest." She pushed the plate toward Samantha. "I've found that once I've accepted responsibility and forgiven myself, I can often turn a negative situation into something positive. We can't undo what's done. We can't change the past. But we can learn from it and maybe use it to make the future better."

"That's good advice." It was a lame response, but it was the best Samantha could do as she considered everything Joy shared.

"I hope it helps. One more thing. Even though it's a choice, forgiving is one of the hardest things we have to do. It's hard enough to forgive another person who has hurt us—it's even harder to forgive ourselves when we've hurt someone else. And for the major things, we may have to forgive over and over. We can't just say, 'Okay, I'm going to forgive myself for that awful thing I did,' and be forever at peace about it. The negative feelings, the anger at yourself, the shame, will come back—often when you least expect them. And when they do, you have to go through the process again."

"Not fun."

"It's not fun, but it's good. I'm sorry, Samantha. I'd love to continue this, but I really have to get back to work. Maybe we can talk more later?"

"Sure. I'll let my friend know what you said."

Joy tapped the table and rose to her feet. "I hope she's able to find some peace."

"Thanks. And thanks for the cookies." Before Joy could walk away, Samantha abruptly asked the question that had been on her mind since yesterday. "By the way, how is Kevin doing? Is he still in the hospital?"

"I don't have much news. I got a couple of texts from Heather, but I haven't spoken with either of them. They know he didn't have a heart attack, so that's good, but they hadn't confirmed a diagnosis. I'm assuming he's still in the hospital. I think Emily's in the store. She might know more."

"I'll stop by there on my way home." And spend some time helping. Maybe while she was doing that, she could pray.

Kevin lay motionless, his eyes closed, trying to visualize anything but the look on Heather's face when she walked out of the hospital room. He was a monster for hurting her, but this new health problem on top of everything else had pushed him almost to a breaking point. Though he should have appreciated her optimism, he didn't. He was angry, bitter, and worried. And he needed his wife at his side, but he had told her to leave.

Where was she?

He reached for his phone and tapped out a text.

I'm sorry. I love you. I need you. Please come back.

He hit "send" then held his phone tightly as if that would speed his message and Heather's response. When it chimed a minute later, he knew before reading her text that she was on her way.

I love you, too. Back in 10.

It was probably less than ten minutes but seemed longer before she came rushing into his room, her face puffy, eyes and nose red from crying. As he held out his arms, she kissed him and stretched out on the bed next to him.

"I'm so sorry. I didn't mean to hurt you." He stroked her hair, cherishing her closeness.

"I know."

"I shouldn't have asked you to leave."

"It's okay. I understand."

"Do you really?"

"Sort of." She raised up on one elbow so she could look at him. "I understand how scary this is for you. It's scary for me and I'm not the one who's sick. But we're in this together, so it hurt me when you said you wanted to be alone."

"As soon as you walked out, I knew I didn't want to be alone." He reached up and stroked her cheek. "It's just—I don't know how we're going to get through this. Another hospital stay. Expensive medications. The baby. I'm supposed to take care of you and I'm stuck shuffling around on a walker like an old man."

"We're supposed to take care of each other. And that's what we're going to do." She kissed him again. "I'm glad you didn't wait much longer before you came to your senses."

"Where did you go?"

"Out to the car. I didn't know what else to do, so I just sat there by myself in the parking lot and cried."

"Oh, Sunshine. I'm a jerk. I'll make it up to you, I promise." He had no idea how but he'd figure it out. "We just have to get through this."

"And we will. It's a bump in the road, that's all."

"You're such an optimist." It was one of the things he loved about her, but right now he didn't want optimism, he wanted action. "Have you heard from Sergeant Grant lately? I wonder if he's making any progress on the investigation."

"No. I guess he doesn't have any news for us."

"I hope he hasn't given up."

"I'm sure he hasn't. He said it could take a while. But even if the case is never solved, it doesn't really matter to us."

"Oh, yes, it does." Kevin's tone was sharper than he intended. He took a breath before he continued. "If the driver was insured, that could pay for my medical costs. And if he has any assets, we could sue him personally for what his insurance doesn't cover—not just medical, but maybe even some of our business losses."

"I hadn't thought about that. Do you want me to call Sergeant Grant?"

"No. Like you said, if he had any news, he'd call us." Kevin moved his hand so it rested on Heather's belly. "How's our little guy doing? Can you feel anything yet?"

"No, silly. It will be another couple of months before I can feel any movement. And don't be so sure it's a boy."

"I'm not. And I don't care what it is. When do you see the doctor?"

"Week after next. Want to go with me?"

"You won't be able to stop me." For a moment, the joy of the new life growing inside Heather filled his heart and mind to the exclusion of all else.

The tap on the door startled them both. "So who's the patient here?" Joy was in the doorway, smirking. "I can come back if you're busy."

"No, come in," Heather said as she slid off the bed. "Your timing is perfect. You can keep Kevin company while I go check on the store."

With a brief acknowledgement of Joy, Kevin focused on Heather. "Are you sure?" He knew she would understand that he was asking if she was okay after having been so upset.

"I'm sure. I also want to stop by the house, then I'll be back for the night." She gave him a light kiss, hugged Joy, grabbed her purse and was out the door.

"Don't get in my wife's way when she's on a mission." Kevin chuckled as he watched her go.

"She's definitely a woman with a purpose." Joy moved to the side of the bed. "How are you doing? All I know is that it wasn't a heart attack."

"We finally got a diagnosis. Pulmonary embolism. It's a blood clot in an artery in my lung. I need to be on blood thinners to dissolve the clot. I'll be in the hospital at least one more night, maybe a little longer. They need to monitor everything closely because I'm still recovering from the closed head injury I got in the crash. Not to mention everything else."

"I'm sorry. You're not getting any breaks, are you?"

"That's an understatement. First the crash, now this. What's next?" Kevin didn't try to hide the bitterness he was feeling.

Joy smiled gently. "You're not really expecting me to answer that, are you?"

"Why not? You always have something wise to say."

"But I can't predict the future."

"You could ask your pal God what He's got in store for me." As soon as the words were out, Kevin realized how rude he sounded. "I'm sorry. I shouldn't have said that—I seem to be doing that a lot lately. Sit down, make yourself comfortable. Or as comfortable as you can be." This room was similar to the one he'd been in before, small and sparsely furnished.

Joy sat in the reclining chair, pushing aside the pillow and blanket Heather had used during the night. "You're right, I could ask God what he's got in store for you. But you could ask him yourself."

"He doesn't seem to be talking to me at the moment." Kevin tried to keep his tone light.

"Maybe you're just not hearing him. It's hard to listen to someone you're angry with."

"You think I'm angry with God?"

"Are you?"

"Angry with God? I don't know. I'm angry, but I'm not even sure there *is* a God, so how can I be angry with him?" Kevin adjusted his blanket and noticed a loose thread. He picked at it to avoid looking at Joy.

"Kevin, I've known you for a long time. I know you believe in God."

"I did. I'm not sure if I do anymore. I don't think the God I believed in would do this to me."

Joy leaned forward and spoke urgently. "Kevin, God didn't do this to you. Someone driving a car and not paying attention did this to you."

"But if there is a God, and if he's truly all-powerful, he could have stopped it."

"Yes. And someday, we'll understand why he didn't. For now, let him help you get through it."

"I'm not finding that so easy." He gave Joy a quick glance then returned his gaze to his blanket. "Heather seems to be the one that's doing okay in that department."

"She could help you, if you'd let her."

"I don't want to tell her how I feel. She thinks we're so blessed because of all the people who are doing things for us. But if we were truly blessed, we wouldn't need all this help."

"Not true." Joy rose and took a few steps, but the room was too small for any serious pacing. "We can be abundantly blessed even when we're going through tough times. In fact, tough times often make us appreciate our blessings more than when times are good."

Even though he wasn't in the mood for platitudes, Kevin backpedaled. "Don't get me wrong. I appreciate the good things. I'm just not sure God's responsible for them."

"Have you told God that?"

"I'm sure he knows how I feel. He's omniscient, right?"

"Of course." Joy returned to the chair. "But by talking to him, you open yourself up for him to help you—for you to understand how he's going to work in your life through the accident and now this."

"Thanks, Joy. I appreciate your help, your friendship. Really." He finally looked at her. "But right now, I'm more focused on how I'm going to get better and how we're going to get our bills paid than I am on figuring out what esoteric meaning this whole situation has."

15

"I'm going to launch a campaign to find the driver who hit me." Kevin shifted on the family room sofa, propped his feet on the coffee table, and opened his laptop. He had been discharged from the hospital that morning. It was great to be home, but he had been told to take it easy and he needed something to do that wouldn't involve a lot of physical exertion. "I know the police are looking, but they obviously need help. I'm going to give it to them."

"And just how are you going to do that?" Heather sat back on her heels, exasperation clear on her face. She had been on the floor arranging his computer's power cord so no one would trip on it.

"I'm going to set up a website and offer a reward."

"Crimeline is already offering a reward."

"But they're not promoting it like I'm going to. And I'm going to offer more money."

"Don't you think that's something you should discuss with me first?" Heather got to her feet.

"Of course. We're discussing it now." He knew she was right. He should have talked with her before announcing his decision. Sheepishly, he continued, "I'm going to set up a Help-Now account so people can donate to the reward. I'll only spend a few hundred dollars of our money to seed the account." His fingers were flying across the keyboard. "I started thinking about this yesterday in the hospital after Joy left.”

“*Joy* gave you this idea?” Heather asked incredulously.

“No. Not directly.” Kevin stopped typing and looked at his wife. “She just got me thinking that maybe there was more that we could be doing to find the piece of garbage that did this to me—to us.”

“Why not just let the police handle it?”

“Why not help them?” He deflected her question, then realized she deserved more from him than a wise guy response. “Look, Sunshine, I’m going to be stuck at home for another four or five days. I’m bored. And I’m angry. I hate that this is happening to us and I feel helpless. I can’t even take care of myself, much less you and the baby. This will make me feel like I’m doing something productive.”

“I know you’re bored. I understand that you’re angry. But you shouldn’t feel helpless. We take care of each other. Right now, I’m taking care of you—with the help of the doctors and nurses. By the time the baby gets here, you’ll be able to take care of us.”

“I love your optimism, Sunshine. I want to believe you’re right. But I need to do this.” He glanced down at his computer, then back up at her. “Want to help?”

With a sigh, Heather sat down next to him on the sofa. “If you’re going to do it anyway, then sure, I’ll help. Tell me the plan.”

“Like I said, I’m going to set up a website. It will have all the details of the crash. Maybe you could go take some pictures of where it happened. I’ll explain my injuries.” He paused. He preferred to keep his medical status private, but he knew it would be necessary to let people know his condition and how long his recovery was going to take. “I’ll talk about the store and how you’re trying to keep it open without me to help run it. And then I’ll say that there are two ways people can help us. One is that if they know something, to call the police. The other is that if they don't know anything but they still want to help, they can contribute to the reward fund. We're not asking them to give money to us. We're asking them to give money to help motivate a snitch."

Heather patted the side of his leg. "What can I do?"

"Help me write the content for the website. Take some pictures. Now I'm sorry I didn't let you take pictures of me while my face was all bruised." Kevin turned his laptop so they could both see the screen, his own enthusiasm rising now that Heather was on board with his idea. "And help me figure out what I haven't thought of yet."

"Here's something to think about. Before you launch the site, let's ask Samantha Lawrence to proofread and edit the content. Emily told me she's majoring in marketing or communications or something like that. She's been such a big help in the store, I'm sure she wouldn't mind doing this."

When Emily explained why she was calling, Samantha almost dropped her phone. Kevin and Heather had built a website to get people to call with tips to find the driver who had hit Kevin. They wanted her to proofread and edit it. For a moment, her throat closed and she couldn't speak.

"Samantha? Are you there?"

"Yes." It was barely a whisper. She coughed and tried again. "Yes, I'm here." Did that sound normal?

"Well, what do you think? I'm sure you're busy, but if I send you the link to the site, could you take a look at it?"

"Um. Sure. Okay." How could she say no? But how could she do this? "Just so you know, finals start next week. I don't have a lot of time right now to do anything but study."

"I understand. I know Kevin and Heather do, too. It's just

that you've been such a huge help in the store. They were hoping you wouldn't mind doing this for them."

"No. No, I don't mind." Of all the lies she'd told in the past month, this had to be the biggest. It was crazy for her to do something to help the police identify her as the hit-and-run driver. But how could she not? "Could you text me the link?"

"Sure. I'll do it right now. And Samantha, thanks so much. I don't know if this is going to help, but it means a lot to Kevin."

Moments later, Samantha was reading the website. It was simple and to the point, with a picture of Kevin using his walker and a picture of where the crash occurred.

Help Find the Hit-and-Run Driver
Who Injured Kevin Wyland

On March 22, shortly after 5 a.m., while riding his bicycle on State Road 434 in Winter Springs, Kevin Wyland was the victim of a hit-and-run driver. The identity of the driver remains unknown.

The injuries Kevin suffered directly from the crash included a spinal fracture that required surgery; a fractured pelvis; broken ribs; a closed head injury; and a broken nose. He later had a pulmonary embolism that was related to the original injuries. Healing is expected to take months and he may never fully recover.

Because the driver has not been identified, arrested, and prosecuted, Kevin and his wife Heather are bearing the full financial burden of lost income and the medical costs his insurance doesn't cover, which are substantial. Bringing the perpetrator to justice would not only get a dangerous driver off the streets, it would also provide Kevin with financial recourse because the driver's insurance would pay his medical bills and he could sue the driver for damages.

If you know anything about this crash, please click here to email us with the details and your contact information.

We are offering a reward for information leading to an arrest.

If you would like to contribute to the reward fund, please click here.

Samantha's heart raced. She hadn't thought about the economic damage she had done to Kevin and Heather beyond the impact of shorter store hours. Even if she had, she couldn't do anything about that now. And it wasn't likely that this website would generate any legitimate leads. The only witness hadn't gotten a good look at her car—the car that was now at the bottom of a lake and was the only thing that could connect her to the crash. And she hadn't told anyone what she'd done. The chances that she would be identified, even with this website out there, were slim.

Closing the site, she tapped out a text to Emily.

Looks good to me.

Kevin was frustrated. Once he'd gotten word through Emily that Samantha thought the website looked good, he began posting it on his social media accounts and asking people to share it. His friends were responding but not at the pace he'd hoped for. On the plus side, several people had made donations to the reward fund.

Closing his laptop, he leaned back and stared out the window into the back yard. Toby lifted his head and woofed softly, then got to his feet and trotted to the front door as the doorbell rang. Kevin picked up his phone to check the image from the doorbell's security camera. Joy was standing on the porch. Using the intercom, he asked, "What are you selling?"

"Ice to Eskimos." Joy waved at the camera. "Are you up to visitors?"

"Absolutely. Do you mind letting yourself in? There's a key under the mat. Heather put it there so I wouldn't have to get up if anyone came by. I'm in the family room." He watched as she retrieved the key and unlocked the door. He heard her greet Toby. A few seconds later, they were both in the family room. "Have a seat. Heather's at the store, so I'm by myself."

"I know. She came in for some tea just as I was leaving the shop."

"Did she ask you to come by?" Kevin would be surprised if she had. At his request, Heather was discouraging visitors. Their pastor had stopped in while he was in the hospital, but others had limited their contact to phone calls and texts.

"No. I've been thinking about our last conversation and wondering if you wanted to talk. Heather said she needed to get some work done in the office while the store is closed and it's always slow at Joyful Cup on Sunday afternoons, so I thought this might be a good time."

Kevin thought back to what they had talked about—how he was feeling angry and doubting God. "So you're here to save my soul?" he quipped.

"Saving souls is above my pay grade. But if I can help you find some peace …" Joy left the sentence unfinished.

"You're a good friend, Joy. I'll find peace when I'm healthy again." He hoped his short response didn't offend her. "Please sit down. Did Heather tell you what we did yesterday?"

"About the website? She mentioned it. How's it going?" She settled into a chair. Toby flopped down next to her.

"Slower than I thought it would. I was hoping it would go

viral right away. Guess that wasn't realistic. Still, we're getting some shares and plenty of encouraging comments, but so far, no tips."

"When did you put it up?"

"Yesterday. Heather and I did most of the work the day before. Then Samantha Lawrence proofed it and last night we started sharing it."

Joy drew a sharp breath. "Samantha proofed it?"

"Yeah. Why do you sound so surprised?"

"Did I sound surprised? I didn't realize you knew her very well."

"It's not like we're best friends. Emily knows her better than Heather and I do. Since the accident, she's been coming into the store a couple of times a week, volunteering. She does a great job with the displays. I'm hoping we'll be able to offer her a part-time position soon. Getting to know her has been one of the few positive things about this whole situation."

"She's a smart young lady. She's been one of my customers ever since she moved in with her grandmother—more often since her grandmother died. I like her."

Kevin recalled his interactions with Samantha. "I think I make her nervous. I don't know why. The first time I saw her after the crash, she left right after Emily introduced us. And I think she had intended to stay at the store longer than that."

"College students can be so unpredictable, can't they?" Joy didn't seem concerned about Samantha's odd behavior. "What did she think about the website?"

"All she said was that it looks good. Emily said she's got finals this week, so I might ask her to take a look at it again later, if we don't find the guy who gives garbage a bad name soon."

Joy sighed. "You still haven't been able to forgive the driver, have you?"

Kevin drew a deep breath and immediately regretted it.

His ribs were still sore. "I thought I had, but that was when I thought I would recover completely."

"What makes you think you're not going to recover completely?"

"The doctor—the cardiologist. She talks about me resuming 'normal' activities and then says I might develop something called exercise intolerance. For me, riding my bike, working out—those are 'normal' activities. But I may not be able to do them."

"That would be due to the pulmonary embolism, right?"

"Sort of. I could get pulmonary hypertension."

Joy bent down to scratch Toby's head. "How is that related to your injuries from the accident?"

"The embolism was likely caused by my inactivity as I'm recuperating. Even the doctor considers it all related."

"I see."

Kevin waited to see if Joy would say anything else, but she didn't. Before the silence could become awkward, he continued, "I know I should be grateful that the crash didn't kill me and that I'm not in a wheelchair. And I *am* grateful for that. But Heather talks about it like it's something to celebrate—I'm just not in the same place. I'm ticked off. I'm ticked off at the driver. I'm ticked off at God. I'm ticked off at—well, at everybody. At the world."

"That's understandable. Most people in your situation would feel the same way. But what are you going to do about it? You can't go through the rest of your life being angry at the world."

"And God."

"God's tough. He can handle your anger. But can you?"

"I don't understand what you mean."

Joy leaned forward, resting her elbows on her knees. "You're feeling angry because you haven't forgiven the driver who hit you. Forgiving the driver will help you let go of the anger." When Kevin snorted, she continued. "When you don't forgive someone who has hurt you, it might feel like you're hurting them, but you're not. You're just hurting yourself—perhaps even more than whatever they did. Can you handle that? Are you willing to let that affect the rest of your life?"

"I'll be fine once they catch the guy." It was all Kevin could think of to say.

"Really? How is that going to change your life? It's not going to undo what happened."

He had the answer to that. "It will give me some legal recourse. If he has insurance or some assets, I can sue and maybe get enough money so we won't be in debt for medical bills for the rest of our lives."

"And if he's found but doesn't have insurance or assets? Will you still be angry?"

"Okay, you got me." Kevin raised his hands in mock surrender. "I don't know. Probably. For a while. I'm sure at some point I'll get over it."

"In the meantime, you're making yourself miserable. You're probably slowing your body's healing process. And you're not helping Heather."

"Helping Heather?" He pounced on the only thing he thought he could defend. "I'm doing everything I can to help her. But there's only so much I can do right now."

"Do you think your anger, your bitterness is good for her? Or the baby?"

"You know about the baby?"

"I guessed. She has all the symptoms."

"She doesn't want to tell anyone yet."

"I understand. I won't say a word. And when she tells me—what do you think? Should I be totally surprised or remind her that I suspected the day she got sick in my shop?"

Heather's voice came from the doorway. "By all means, give me a big, fat 'I told you so!'" She entered the room with her purse on one shoulder and grocery bags in each hand. Dropping everything on the floor, she leaned over to kiss Kevin and smiled at Joy. "Some watchdog we have. Toby, you could have at least greeted me." Then, to Kevin and Joy, "Do I want to know why you two are talking about the baby?"

"Joy is giving me some of her usual wise counsel." It was as much of an answer as Kevin wanted to give. "What have you been doing?"

"End of the week chores. Paid some bills. Checked the inventory, placed some orders. Stopped at Publix." Heather held her hand to her mouth as she yawned. "Sorry. It's not the company. I'm just tired most of the time."

Joy stood, pulling her car key from her pocket. "That goes with being pregnant. It won't last. Sit down. Take a nap. Can I put the groceries away for you?"

"No, thanks. I didn't get much. It won't take me a minute."

The two women embraced briefly and Joy patted Kevin's hand. "I hope the website works out for you. Take care." Was it his imagination or did her eyes add, "And think about our conversation"?

Exams were over. Samantha didn't want to think about what her grades were likely to be.

Why couldn't she get off this emotional roller coaster? She ricocheted between feeling guilty about what she'd done and thankful that she hadn't been caught, between wishing there was more she could do for Kevin and Heather and being proud of how much she'd done for them, between being unable to eat or sleep and bingeing on junk food and sleeping for ten to twelve hours at a stretch.

Her friends had to know that something wasn't right. She had ignored messages and declined enough invitations that they had given up. The only friend who was still trying was Amber, but Samantha couldn't forget that she had been sending a text to Amber when the accident happened. When she looked at Amber, she saw Kevin landing on her windshield. Fortunately, Amber had gone home for the summer. Maybe by the time she got back, Samantha would have put the accident behind her.

Before the accident, Samantha had considered taking the summer off from school as well, but decided not to. When Gram was alive, the plan was for Samantha to attend classes year-round so she could graduate early. When Gram died, Samantha and her mother agreed she should stay on her original schedule. So here she was with nearly two weeks of nothing to do before the summer semester started. Nothing to do, that is, but think.

Joy's words played over and over in Samantha's mind. *When people feel guilty about something, they usually want to fix the situation. They focus on the person they harmed. They want to correct their mistake.*

We can't change the past. But we can learn from it and we might be able to use it to make the future better.

How could she possibly use what she'd done to Kevin to make the future better? When was it going to stop haunting her? Could it really help to pray?

From their patio, Kevin and Heather watched Toby romp in the backyard. In a few more weeks the summer heat would kick in, but right now the weather was ideal for being outside. Kevin had been out of the hospital a week and a half. Today he'd had a checkup with his orthopedist and Heather had her first prenatal visit.

Heather rested her hands on her still flat belly as if she were cradling the tiny creature she carried. "It's been a good news day, hasn't it? The baby and I are doing fine, the morning sickness shouldn't last much longer, and you can stop using the walker."

"We need to tell my mother and sister about the baby." Kevin knew his mother would be beside herself with excitement about her first grandchild.

"We need to invite your mom for a visit."

"Can you handle having her here?" Kevin's experience with pregnant women was mostly second-hand stories about cravings and hormones. Would Heather be able to handle a houseguest, even a family member that she loved?

"If we can delay it for a few weeks until I'm past the morning sickness and you're a little stronger, sure. I know it's been driving her crazy to not be here with you, but I get so tired."

"I know. When she finds out about the baby, she'll understand. I'll call her tomorrow and see if she wants to come in a month or so. That'll give her something to look forward to."

As they sat in comfortable silence, Kevin thought Heather had never looked more beautiful. And he realized that he hadn't even thought about the hit-and-run driver all day.

In spite of Heather's concerns, Kevin insisted he was able to work in the store for a few hours each day. "I can walk on my own, I can talk to customers, and Emily's there to help if anything needs to be lifted. I'll be fine. We have to get back on this horse."

He knew Heather was thinking about the last time he was in the store. So was he. The memory of the excruciating chest pains, of Heather telling him he would be okay, of being loaded into the ambulance on a stretcher was all too fresh for both of them. But that wasn't going to happen again and he needed to get back to work.

Business was slow—not unusual for a Tuesday morning. Emily was stocking shelves while Heather worked in the office. When the door opened, Kevin looked up from behind the counter with a smile, which broadened when he recognized Samantha. She spoke before he had a chance to greet her.

"Finals were last week and I've got some free time. Is there anything I can help you with?" Samantha waved at Emily as she approached Kevin.

"I feel like we're taking advantage of you. I wish we could afford to pay you."

"I'm offering to help and I'm not expecting to get paid." Samantha looked down as she traced the edge of the counter with her index finger. "Are you back at work now?"

"On a limited basis. I still have to take it easy."

A small display of refrigerator magnets set up near the

cash register captured Samantha's attention. Kevin recalled Emily telling him that she would usually just look around the store, spot something that needed to be done, and do it. As Samantha neatened the magnets, she said, "I didn't realize how badly you'd been hurt until I read the copy for your website."

"I hope you got my message thanking you for taking a look at that. Heather took some marketing courses in college, but we both thought you would have a better eye for it than we did."

"I don't know about that. I thought you did a good job with it." She glanced at him briefly and turned back to rearranging the magnets. "These are cute. Have you gotten any leads?"

"No. We've received some donations for the reward fund and a lot of positive comments, but no actual leads." Kevin thought she seemed more comfortable with him than she had the last time they'd talked, but she still didn't seem completely relaxed.

"And the police don't have anything?"

"Not yet." Kevin hadn't discussed the crash in detail with anyone besides Heather and Joy, but he didn't want Samantha to feel like he was shutting her out. "There was only one witness and he didn't get a good look at the car. And it could take another month or so for the lab to finish analyzing the debris they found at the scene."

"Will that help them find the driver?"

"Maybe. It will tell them what kind of car it was. If they can find the car, they should be able to find the driver." The door to the store opened and Kevin looked past Samantha to call a greeting at a middle-aged woman carrying a small dog.

"So they haven't closed the case." It was half statement, half question.

"No, they haven't. But I don't know how high on their list of priorities it is." He started to excuse himself to go help the customer who had just walked in, but Emily was a step ahead of him. He turned back to Samantha. "I do know the car that hit me was red because it left some paint on my bike."

"You got your bike back?"

"Yeah. It's damaged beyond repair, but I wanted it back. I keep it on our patio as a reminder."

"I wouldn't think you'd need a reminder. I don't know how you could ever forget something like that." She moved from the magnets to a display of pet fragrances. "Do people really put perfume on their dogs?"

"You'd be surprised at how well that sells. The nail polish is popular, too."

"My dog back in Ohio is a big, clumsy mutt. I couldn't imagine putting nail polish on him. But I like this color." She held up one of the bottles as they both chuckled. "Are you going to get a new bike?"

"I don't know. It's going to be a while before I can even think about riding again." He managed to keep his tone neutral, to not let his pain come through his voice.

She seemed to hesitate a moment before asking, "If you get any leads from the website, will you follow up on them?"

"Me personally? No. I'll pass them along to Sergeant Grant, the investigator on the case. I'm not going to play amateur detective. Besides, I'm starting to accept that the driver may never be found. It bothers me, because I'd like to see him get justice, but I'm not as angry about it as I was." His words surprised himself. Why was he sharing these private feelings with someone he barely knew when he hadn't shared them with Heather yet?

"I guess that means you're healing emotionally as well as physically. Do you ever talk to Joy at Joyful Cup? I think she would tell you to try to find some good in the situation, to figure out how God can work through you to turn this into something positive."

"Yes, I talk to Joy, and that sounds like something she

would say. I just haven't figured out how to make this a positive thing." It was his turn to feel uncomfortable. This wasn't a conversation he wanted to have with a young woman he barely knew, no matter how helpful she'd been to him.

"Maybe you could do something to help other people who have been injured in bike accidents." Samantha replaced the bottle of nail polish in the display box as the woman Emily had been helping came to the counter with her purchases. "Let me get out of your way. I'll go redo that display." She gestured to a utilitarian stack of dog treats.

Kevin watched her briefly before he turned his attention to the customer in front of him. He scratched her dog's head. "Hello, there. Is this everything?"

As he exchanged pleasantries with the customer and processed her purchase, Samantha's words played in his mind.

Turn this into something positive.

Help other people who have been injured in bike accidents.

With Lucy on her lap, Samantha sat on the window seat in her bedroom, staring unseeingly down onto the street.

Had Kevin given her a pass today when he said that he was accepting that the driver may never be found? Barely a week ago, he was trying to create a social media storm to drive people to his website so they could leave tips on who the driver was. Today he seemed calm and accepting. And if he didn't care if she were identified and arrested, what did that mean for her? Would she be able to finally put this behind her and move on? Or would the guilt always be there, creeping into her consciousness when she was least expecting it?

Adding to her guilt was the fact that Kevin and Heather had obviously come to trust her and even depend on her. She had betrayed them by leaving the scene of the crash and was continuing to betray them by her silence. And what support she'd given them by occasionally volunteering in their store was a pittance compared to what they could probably get from her insurance company if they knew who she really was.

Joy was right. She wanted to correct her mistake. But was she strong enough to do it?

She picked up her phone and tapped out a text.

Got almost 2 weeks before classes start. Can you come for a visit?

It only took a few minutes before her mother answered.

Do you want to come home?

Going home sounded wonderful but only if she could turn back the clock, and she couldn't.

Can't leave Lucy.

She hoped her mother wouldn't suggest boarding the cat. To do what she had to do, she couldn't leave town.

Let me see what I can do. I'll let you know. Love you.

Moving Lucy off her lap, Samantha slid to her knees and prayed.

Kevin and Heather were taking Toby for an after-dinner walk through the neighborhood. Heather insisted on holding the leash so the dog wouldn't jerk Kevin's arm if he tried to chase a squirrel. After walking almost a block in companionable silence, Kevin spoke. "I've been thinking."

"Should I be concerned?" Heather teased.

"Always." He smiled, then became serious. "Do you ever think about what might have happened if I had been killed in the accident?"

"No." Heather's response was quick. "The day it happened, I was scared. It wasn't that I thought about you dying, I was just scared about how badly you were hurt. Then when I knew you were going to be okay, I was grateful and focused on helping you get better. Do you think about it?"

"Not often, but I have. I've thought about you being pregnant and having a baby and me not being here with you."

She stopped and put her hand on his arm. "Look at me. You didn't die. Don't think like that. You're here with me. We're having this baby together."

"I know, Sunshine. Believe me, I'm not obsessing over dying. But Samantha was in the store this morning and she said something I've been thinking about all day." He paused, scanning the twilight sky for the right words. "I'm trying to make some sense out of all this."

"What did Samantha say?"

"She was talking about turning this into something positive. About maybe finding a way to help other people who had been in bike crashes. And it made me think about who would have helped you if I wasn't here."

"We're blessed to have friends and a wonderful church family here. They would have helped. And we have family— your mom and sister, my brother—even if they don't live close by."

"Yeah, I know. That's not my point. My point is, what about the people who don't have friends and family like we do? Who helps them when something like this happens?"

"I don't know." She slid her hand down his arm, laced her fingers with his, and began walking again.

"Maybe we need to figure that out." There. He'd finally said it out loud.

"Maybe we do." She squeezed his hand and he knew she would support him, wherever this idea took them.

Samantha spotted her mother in the crowd of people waiting

for their rides at the curbside pickup level of Orlando International Airport. She navigated through the traffic and found a place to park just a car length away. Jumping out of the car, she ran to embrace her mother, hoping she would be able to hold back the tears as her emotions threatened to overwhelm her.

"I'm so glad to see you. Did you have a good flight? Here, let me get that." She reached for the handle of her mother's suitcase.

"You look tired, love. I think you need a break." Connie Lawrence surrendered her luggage to her daughter.

"It was a tough semester." The understatement of the year. "Come on, let's get out of here."

"You're driving Gram's car?"

"Yeah. I didn't want it to just sit. And a friend of mine needed a car, so I loaned her mine." Samantha was able to avoid eye contact as she slammed the trunk closed. That should be one of the last lies she would tell. It would keep her mother from asking questions when she didn't see Samantha's car at home. "I hope you don't mind."

"Of course not. It's your car. And there's no reason not to use this one until we decide what to do with it." Connie settled into the passenger's seat and snapped her seatbelt. "Want to go somewhere delicious and fun for dinner?"

Samantha was briefly occupied with maneuvering past all the other vehicles that were in various stages of picking up passengers. Once away from the terminal, she responded. "Actually, I went to the grocery store this morning. I thought we could stay home and cook something together."

"Sounds good to me. We need to catch up."

"I know. I'm sorry I haven't called much lately."

"It's okay, love. I know you're busy with school. But I miss you."

"I miss you, too. Tell me how everybody is." She wanted

to keep her mother talking so she would have to say as little as possible tonight.

"Okay, that's done." With a few more taps on the keyboard, Kevin turned to Heather with a look of satisfaction on his face. They were both at their desks in the bedroom they used as a home office. "The website is down and I've redirected the domain name to a page on our store site that asks people to either check back for more information or to email us if they have an immediate question. Later, we'll put the details about the foundation on that page."

Heather saved the file she was working on. "What are you going to do about the donations to the reward fund?"

"I'm going to send everybody an email tomorrow. I'll explain that we're just going to let the police handle the investigation and that we're working on setting up an organization to help others who are victims of hit-and-run drivers. I'll offer to refund their money immediately or ask if they'd like to wait until we've figured out exactly what we're going to do and maybe help us with that by letting us transfer their money to the foundation." The anger that had been his constant companion since the accident was fading, replaced with ideas that were swirling in his head. They could raise money to help people with expenses. They could recruit and screen volunteers who could help with the things that families of people in the hospital needed. They could find ways to provide long-term support for people who suffer life-changing injuries. Most important, they would help the children of those injured or killed by hit-and-run drivers.

"I think everyone who contributed to the reward fund would probably rather have their money used that way."

"I hope so." He got to his feet and pulled her to him. "I don't know exactly how we're going to do this or how much we'll be able to do, but we'll figure it out."

"Yes, we will. God will show us the way."

Kevin drew a deep breath, savoring Heather's sweet fragrance and the peace that surrounded them both. "I think you're right."

It had been a perfect morning. Samantha and Connie had walked to Joyful Cup for coffee then strolled around Town Center as Samantha pointed out all of Gram's favorite places. On their way home, they stopped back in Joyful Cup to pick up some cookies to snack on later. Joy was behind the counter, so Samantha was able to introduce them. She hoped she hadn't overdone it by telling her mom about how wise Joy was, but she wanted Connie to know where to go for support if she needed it.

As the two women finished lunch at home, Connie said, "What would you like to do this afternoon?"

That was the opening Samantha needed. "I have to run an errand. Why don't you just stay here and relax? This shouldn't take long."

"Maybe I'll take a nap. We stayed up later than I'm used to last night."

"Sorry."

"Don't be. I loved it. We can do it again tonight."

Samantha didn't respond. She grabbed her phone and the key to Gram's car, hugged her mother, murmured, "I love you," and left the house.

It only took about ten minutes for her to reach her destination, but she wasn't sure how long she sat in the parking lot once she got there. Finally she drew a deep breath, got out of the car, and entered the building.

A receptionist smiled from behind a panel of bullet-proof glass. "May I help you?"

"Yes." Her voice was clear and confident. "I hit a man on a bicycle about six weeks ago and left the scene. I'd like to turn myself in, please."

Joy was cleaning one of the coffee urns when the scene of Kevin's accident suddenly flashed into her mind. The memory of the emergency lights, the helicopter, and the chill she felt were as vivid as they were on the morning it happened. Then a sense of peace enveloped her. Everything was fine now.

The door to the shop opened. Joy looked up and smiled.

Epilogue

After turning herself in at the police station, Samantha was arrested and spent the night in jail. The following day, she was released on bail, which her mother arranged.

Kevin and Heather were shocked when Sergeant Grant told them the identity of the hit-and-run driver. Several conversations with Joy helped them deal with their feelings of anger and betrayal and begin the process of forgiving Samantha.

Against her attorney's advice, Samantha wrote a heartfelt letter of apology to the Wylands, saying how sorry she was and offering only minimal explanation and no excuses for her actions. She wasn't surprised when the Wylands did not immediately respond. After sending the letter, she stayed away from the Wylands' store as she focused on preparing herself to deal with the legal consequences of the crash.

Several months later, her attorney reached a plea agreement with the state attorney that included 60 days in the county jail and five years supervised probation during which time she had to perform community service that included speaking to high school and college students about the dangers of texting while driving. In addition, her driver's license was suspended and she was ordered to pay restitution to Kevin. Because she had no criminal record, she would have avoided jail time had she not tampered with evidence by dumping her car in a lake.

When Kevin and Heather heard about the sentence, they

asked Joy to arrange a meeting with Samantha before she reported to jail. They told Samantha they had forgiven her and invited her to work with their fledgling ministry when she was released from jail.

Following a surprisingly short period of negotiations, Kevin reached a settlement with Samantha's insurance company that paid his medical bills and reimbursed some of his economic damages. A year after the accident, he was deemed fully recovered. Kevin and Heather continued to run their store, had a healthy baby boy, and built a small local ministry that assists victims and families of hit-and-run crashes.

Samantha was suspended from school following her arrest. After completing the incarceration portion of her sentence, she applied for and received a waiver to resume her education and was able to graduate two years after the crash. In her free time, she volunteered with the Wylands' ministry.

Joy maintained her friendships with Kevin, Heather, and Samantha as the next Joyful Cup story unfolded.

Is your book club reading *Choices*?

Visit **JoyfulCupStory.com** for more information about the Joyful Cup Story series and to download a list of questions to guide your book club's discussion.

Acknowledgments

The idea for *Choices* first came to me more than five years ago. Though I've written (or ghostwritten) more than thirty non-fiction books, the process of writing a novel was both intriguing and intimidating. Once I voiced my desire, my wonderful husband Jerry Clement became my biggest champion, encouraging and even nagging me along the way as I talked but didn't write. And when I finally began to write, he listened, offered suggestions, and proofread. Every time I voiced a doubt, he shot it down. As the manuscript neared completion, he designed the cover and supported me through the myriad of details that are essential to finishing and publishing a book. Had it not been for him, *Choices* would not be in your hands today.

My deepest appreciation goes out to so many others who helped as I was formulating, researching, and finalizing the story. They include:

The excellent medical professionals who answered my questions in meetings, on the phone, and even at parties. Paul A. Dowdy, MD, is an orthopedic surgeon who was the victim of a hit-and-run driver that, as of this writing, has not been caught. I had already begun work on *Choices* when my cousin introduced me to Paul, who was immediately generous with his time, explaining the type of injuries and complications Kevin would likely have suffered. Other doctors who shared their expertise were Michael M. Bibliowicz, DO, an ENT-otolaryngologist who is both a personal friend and an amazing doctor; Regan A. Schwartz, MD, who specializes in emergency medicine and took the time to talk with me at his son's graduation party; and Brian K. Dublin, MD, my father's cardiologist.

Other medical professionals I need to thank are Virginia Bibliowicz, a dear friend and former nurse (who is also my unofficial PR/marketing manager); Betty Jacobs, my daughter-in-law's mother and a respiratory therapist; Sandee Pangonis, friend and ER nurse. Big thanks also go to my cousin, Stephen Rooks, who is the director of respiratory therapy at a Colorado hospital and has also been the victim of a car-versus-bicycle crash (fortunately, *not* a hit-and-run).

Winter Springs Police Chief Kevin Brunelle patiently explained what happens at the crash scene and how the follow-up investigation is handled. Assistant State Attorney Domenick Leo told me how the prosecution and plea agreement process works.

Other friends who shared their knowledge and expertise so I could write an authentic story include Jackie Daly, who helped me write Samantha's texts; Amanda Grow, who explained how the 911 system in Seminole County works; and Kristine Shrauger, who answered my questions about UCF. Friends who shared pictures of their favorite coffee mugs for Joyful Cup characters to use include James Cressler, Ann Marshall, Annette Meeks, Karyl Melick, Candy Morgan, Kyla Perry, Kara Snyder, Tina Yeager, and a few others I'm sure I've missed.

On the writing craft side, thanks to all my fellow Word Weavers who critiqued the manuscript in progress and the members of the local chapter of American Christian Fiction Writers who provided tips and encouragement. I appreciate the education provided by the faculty at the Florida Christian Writers Conference, especially Zena Dell Lowe, a writer, director, and filmmaker who taught an excellent class on Hollywood story-telling tools. My beta readers—Susan Baccus, Virginia

Bibliowicz, and Lisa Hurley—gave me thoughtful, detailed input as the manuscript was nearing completion.

Finally, there's Mark Goldstein, president of the Central Florida Christian Chamber of Commerce, whose enthusiasm for this project imposed a hard deadline for getting the book finished and published. My gratitude for that is beyond words.

In addition to those who have played a specific role in the creation of this novel are the family members and friends who have supported and encouraged me every step of the way. I am so blessed by and thankful for them and you, dear reader. May you know God's peace and mercy always.

JACQUELYN LYNN finds joy in her faith, family and friends, as well as in the knowledge that she is living God's purpose for her life. She is the author of more than 30 books, including *Finding Joy in the Morning: You* can *make it through the night* and *Words to Work By: 31 devotions for the workplace based on the book of Proverbs*. She is also the co-creator of a series of Christian coloring books for adults. *Choices* is her first novel and the first in the Joyful Cup Story series. She lives in Winter Springs, Florida, where the Joyful Cup stories are based.

Connect with Jacquelyn at CreateTeachInspire.com, where you'll find links to join her email list and engage with her on social media.

Use the *Finding Joy Journal* to help you keep track of
what brings you joy, let go of what doesn't, and guide
you along your own joyful journey.

Available on Amazon and wherever books are sold.

Color Your Faith!

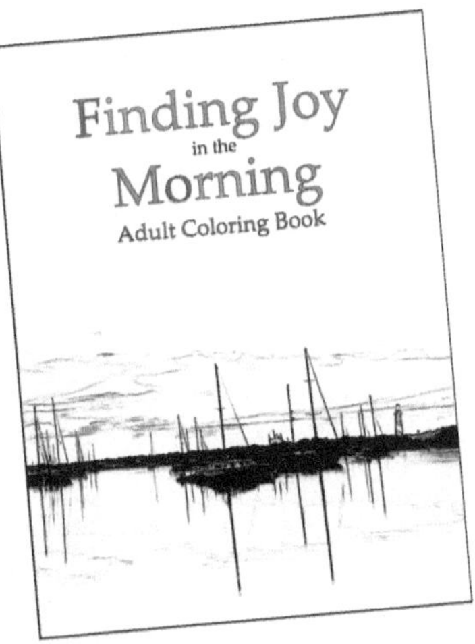

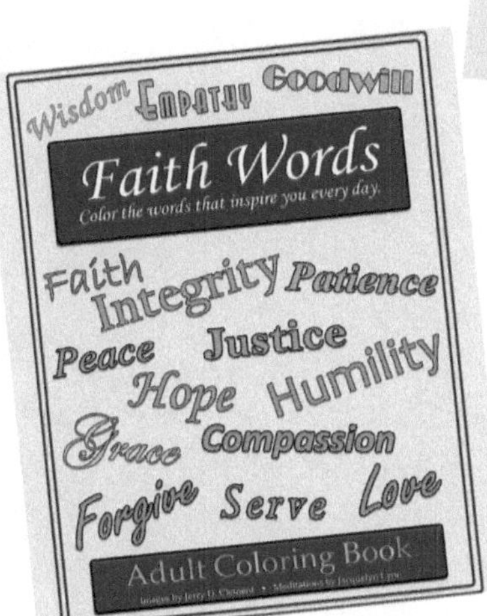

Available on Amazon.

Messages of inspiration and motivation based on the teachings of the world's greatest business advisor: King Solomon.

Devotions ideal for beginning your work day, opening a meeting, or just taking a break.

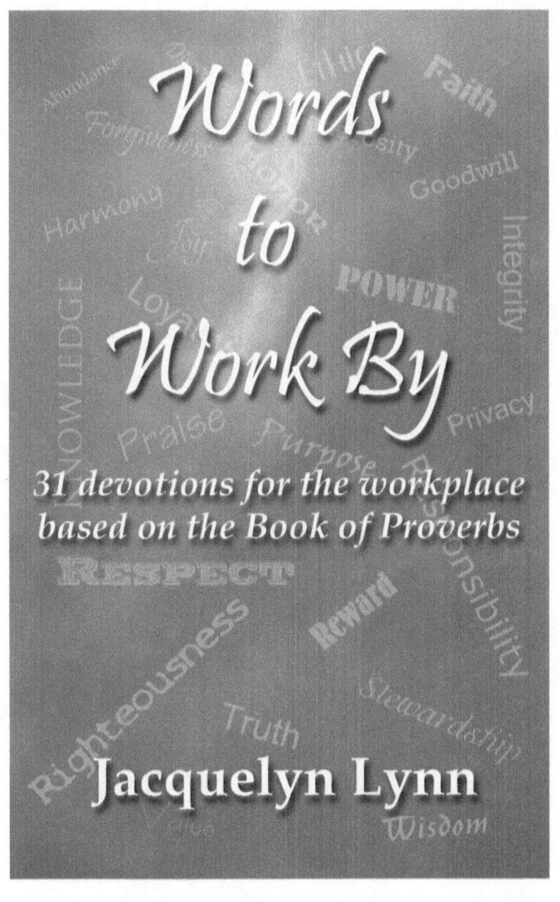

Available on Amazon.